QUICKIES!

|||||||||||||||||||||||||||||||

BY DJ ASS MAGGOTS

|||||||||||||||||||||||||||||||||||||

ISBN: 0615698336
ISBN 13: 9780615698335
Library of Congress Control Number: 2013901893
CreateSpace Independent Publishing Platform
Zandpour, Hermosa Beach, CA

CONTENTS

||||||||||||||||||||||||

II. New York 93

III. Grenada 123

PSYCHO

THE ONE-PAGERS
‖‖‖‖‖‖‖‖‖‖‖‖‖‖‖‖‖‖‖‖‖‖‖‖

It's all about the one-pagers.
Fuck writing short stories, novels, poems, or anything else.

With one-pagers, you're done when you walk away.
I hate trying to recreate moods, develop characters.

I think of my reader, my audience, as a one-night stand.
No need to develop rapport. No page-turning here.
Just a quick fix, a quick thrust and out.

No need for paragraphs.

I've run out of shit to say.
Let's make this one a half-pager.

November 22, 2002

MASTER CONVERSATIONALIST
|||||||||||||||||||||||||||||||||||||||||

I'm a master conversationalist. I can get into a conversation with anyone about anything. You see, there is a magic combination of words that will get people talking. It's different for everyone. The trick is to gather enough background and environmental clues to spark their interest. They don't give a shit what the other person has to say. They just want to talk, and talk, and talk. Some kind of cathartic, self-psychoanalytical release.

So why be a master conversationalist? What is the point, really?

Ever wanted a job? Hate interviews? Ever wanted to get into someone's pants?

If you have the key to someone's mind, you can open them, just like I'm doing to you.

See how easy it is?

August 21, 2004

I'm "Gooing"
||||||||||||||||

An empty sheet...

You give me a page and expect me to write out my life. My pleasure. My pain.

It's not that easy.

I'm a philosopher now. My battles are with thoughts, not with words. Most of these ideas are never captured on paper. I will never be prolific.

So sublime I've felt recently. I want to live forever! And yet, so morose. I want to kill myself! But I can't write.

It's not me; it's the language. English is so limiting. For example, what is the word that describes the feeling just before an orgasm? There isn't a word for that...in any language.

I wish I were a Martian.

August 20, 2004

PARTY #69
||||||||||||||

The two sinister witches leered down at me and continued their incessant laughter. They had somehow perched themselves a few steps above me on the only stairwell in the castle. Strategically positioned, the dastardly witches had blocked access to the second floor, which contained the Rumpus Room, Game Room, Master Parlor, and two bedrooms, and the Master Parlor.

"My, my, my. You ladies look lovely this evening. Do you come here often? What's your sign? Haven't we met before?"

"Oh my God," the tall witch answered first. "Is that, like, a line or something?"

"My dear. That was my humble attempt at making a mockery of all pick-up lines and putting a smile on your face, all at the same time."

"Don't try to act smart," the short witch blurted. "'Cause you're not!" She then whispered something to the other one, and the two of them began laughing hysterically, pointing at me and cackling all the while.

Now the tall one attacked. "Who are you, anyways? You look like some kind of wanna-be pimp."

"Actually, tonight I envision myself as a swordsman. A hero warrior battling witches and warlocks, while dodging dungeons and dragons, all within the confines of this glorious castle."

"Hmphhh..." the tall witch retorted, "you're more like a court jester or a clown of some kind." The two burst forth with another round of giggles.

With my best impression of a British accent, I returned fire. "Your sarcasm, if I may call it such, does not become you, my fellow droogies."

"What are you talking about?" the short one whined.

"Look, my wit is clearly wasted on you two pseudo-adolescent mental midgets. I did want to get up those stairs, but now I am so thoroughly disgusted I'll resign myself to the first floor. Your two-cent insults have gone *unnoticed*. Adieu."

And with that, I stumbled off, forgetting about the witches instantaneously. My heart was pumping now. I could feel it squeeze like a sponge, pulsating blood to my fingers and toes. As I walked down the hall, images became disturbing. The shadows of flickering candles told the tale of dragons dancing with hobgoblins. I opened the door to a room and saw the grim reaper inside, licking his lips at me. This door, I closed quickly.

I walked into the backyard. Various heathens were mulling about, drinking beer, and talking about the merits of existential philosophers. All of a sudden, my heart stopped and I fell to the ground. All went black.

They say that, the second before you die, your whole life flashes before your eyes. That's bullshit. I didn't get a chance to think of anything. One minute I was feeling great, enjoying life, feeling alive. The next minute I was dead. There might have been a minute in between when a paramedic was telling another paramedic to compress my chest harder, in order to get the blood to pulsate to the fingers and toes. Nevertheless, it's all over now.

The moral of the story is this: stop reading stories, and go out there and fuck someone.

August 13, 2000

IMAGINE
||||||||||

The moment had finally come. No one was around, so I stripped off my clothes and ran naked into the field. The slipping and sliding of my feet on the soft, wet grass was the only baptism I'd ever had. I met a large gray squirrel who beckoned me deeper into the forest. It led me to a sparkling stream deep within the jungle darkness. Here, many other animals had gathered and were peacefully frolicking. Lions and tigers were holding hands. Cats and dogs were playing volleyball. Some Israelis and Palestinians were busy building a tree house.

"This is fantastic!" I exclaimed.

Just then, the squirrel stuck out its foot. I tripped and my face landed in cow shit.

Everyone laughed at me...

March 18, 1996

ALLITERATION ON AMERICAN AIRLINES

Broken and busted,
Brazened burlesque-show boy.
Beaten and bitter,
Back down you go, boy.

Cynical and jaded,
Do the trees block your breeze?
Whether loved or hated,
See the ease in your teasing sleaze.

Mince no words with me,
My mental cavalry bleeds to poke at thee.
Let me pounce and trounce,
You pathetic half-once bounce.

September 1997

THE PITCH
IIIIIIIIIIII

"All right, I've got an idea!"

"Yeah?"

"We'll do a hiking bit."

"And?"

"Except that it won't be a regular hiking story. It'll be kind of funny—with wacky antics."

"And?"

"And...we'll...We'll throw in three characters that you would never expect to be in the same story. Yeah...Yeah, that's it."

"Who are the characters?"

"The characters...uh...um. OK. This guy Kent who I went to school with."

"Sounds pretty exciting."

"No, it'll be good. This guy Kent, he was like a granola boy. All about the outdoors. A hiker. Tree hugger and all that shit. He would wear hiking boots to class and eat trail mix."

"Who else?"

"Who else? Uh...mmm...a mobster. Italian. Sylvio, from the *Sopranos*. Yeah, that's it. Picture him on the hike with his three-piece Italian suit, talking about killing somebody."

"A mobster and a granola boy on a hike...hmm...Who else?"

"A rapper. A real good rapper. He'll rap while they hike. We'll need the best...Tupac. Yeah, Tupac."

"Tupac? Isn't he dead?"

"No, no, no. He's in hiding. He won't reveal his identity. He'll call himself 'Mak.'"

"So you wanna do a story about three hikers—Kent, the granola boy; Silvio, the mobster from the *Sopranos*; and the late superstar rapper Tupac Shakur. You must be fuckin' kidding me!"

"Not at all, sir. It'll be great. Think of the audience cross-section."
"Hmm...yeah...OK. I can't believe I'm gonna let you do this. All right, give me five thousand words on my desk, Monday morning. Then we'll see if this is truly worth prime-time television."
"Thank you, sir. You won't regret this. Thank you, sir."
"Now get the fuck out of my office. And close the door behind you. "
"Thank you, sir."

December 28, 2002

Veins of Espresso
||||||||||||||||||||||||||||

How quickly I'm alive again...
I was down, but now I'm fucking found.
This is the last night on earth,
So grind, smile, and scream for all its worth.

Look in my eyes...Look in *my* eyes.
This is my life, my life, my life.
Forget the rest, Jimi said it best...

"I'm the one that has to die
When it's time for me to die,
So let me live my life
The way I want to."

More than just "carpe diem" or "seize the day"
More than "do not go gentle into that good night,"
More than "rage, rage against the dying of the light"

I am fucking life up the ass
Like it's an expensive whore,
Getting all I can from it
And leaving life on its belly, exhausted,
Dripping in sweat and excrement...
Begging for a wheelchair!

And if all this amuses you,
Good.
And if you felt even just a trace of emotion,
Good.

Apparently, you're not dead yet.

January 24, 1997

RAMBLINGS OF AN OUTCAST
||||||||||||||||||||||||||||||||||

My old friend is back.
"Sorrow," I began to wonder.
Work your filth
On to my new rags.

Another late night with the poems.
Thanks to my friend, Sorrow.
My claim to obscurity.
Mad, sad, not glad; bad, very sad.

Ah, youth! Rejoice in your wetness and muscles
Break me open
Eat me out alive. Eat me alive.
The monster's mouth drips.
The RED of her monthly injury,
The WHITE of his one-eyed snake,
The BLUES of hu"MAN"ity

Glory, glory, glory, hallelujah!
God shed her grace on thee.

August 19, 1993

BEHNAM: A GARDEN-VARIETY POET

Who am I?
What am I?
Am I Popeye?
Not quite.

I am a garden-variety man with AB+ blood,
A simple statistic in an equation.
Another anonymous baby.
Another boring death.

I shall live a standard life.
A college degree, a respectable job.
Maybe I'll raise a litter.
We'll live in a safe, family-oriented community.

Or maybe I'll defer the bondage of marriage
For the handcuffs of dating.
Promiscuity with coworkers and friends,
Until they all depart for future husbands.

Ah, the tragic life of the lonely artist.
Romantic, yet this is not my fate,
For I do not have the talent.
This is quite obvious in my garden-variety poetry.
Maybe I will become a great leader,
Helping my community, my country, or my planet,
But I fear, once again, I lack the talent.
Ambition and confidence have left me long ago.

I prefer to wallow in my own pity.
I am singing into the morose mud of melancholia.
My alliteration is poor, my metaphors are trite.
Am I a generic label of a brand name?

As I reread the previous stanzas,
I find that this poem makes me gag.
Where is the talent?
Nothing but whining.

Are most generic poets this self-conscious?
What type of audience responds to this type of poetry?
Have these words captured my personality?
Do I have a personality worth capturing?

Indeed, others have written such poetry.
However, this poem is mine.
These are the true workings inside my head.
I have created.

My parents have named me Behnam
Probably not a name to be recorded in history.
But I have skin, and bones, and AB+ blood.
By random chance, I am Persian American.

When the mugger pulls out her gun
Will he care who I am?
Behnam—a human being,
A garden-variety poet with AB+ blood.

July 4, 1993

PUERTO VALLARTA '99
|||||||||||||||||||||||||||||||||

"Enjoy the power and beauty of your youth.
Floss. Stretch. Dance.
Get to know your parents."

"Live in New York City once,
But leave before it makes you hard.
Live in Northern California once,
But leave before it makes you soft."

"Don't mess with your hair too much."

"Wear sunscreen."

"Upside, inside out,
Livin' la Vida loca."

Fuck New York City (FNYC).
Fuck U.N.I.T.Y.

We like to party. We like to party.
We like to party. We like to party.

Happiness is just around the corner.

Fuck New York City.
Is your life upside down?
Negative energy.
Negative energy.

No scrubs? No hoochie bitches.
Are you hungry?
Do you want a Hot Pocket? An Eggo?

Viva Mexico!

Love or death?

As your attorney, I advise you to end this poem.

August 1999

AN OPEN MIND
||||||||||||||||||||

War is peace. Oh well, around we go.
Stay away from me. My bolts are loose.
See the bee. It stings and then it dies.
Finally, the TV has raped my mind.

Who am I and who are you?
Others have made us, and yes, they'll shape us.
Break free and lose your grip.
Let go of the human rope.

Insanity has come for you and me.
Good-bye, dear old planet Earth.

And some brains on the sidewalk.
I know what you mean.
And some brains in the kitchen sink.
I know just what you mean.

And my mind was so open my brain spilled on the ground.

1992

SOUTH CENTRAL
|||||||||||||||||||||

The ramblings of red paint:
Crenshaw mafia, Crenshaw mafia.
On every wall, every single wall.
The art of the modern gangster.

Today, a project begins in the "projects"
To clean, renew, and soothe.
Taggers with guns await nightfall
Crenshaw nights all over again.

DJ lives on 130th Street,
A young man dodging bullets to school.
We clean and paint his shanty.
"Thank you," he says, and he means it.

There are kind and gentle people in hell.
I know because I've met one.
This is so, so very wrong.
Is heaven reserved for slave drivers in Washington?

Back in suburbia,
The soft, chubby hands of the rich
Poke and prod the buttons of a clever machine.
Channel 2, Channel 4, Channel 7.

A lady with a plastic nose and plastic breasts
Falls asleep to an unfamiliar war movie
Known to some as the eleven o'clock news,
As DJ lies dead in his Crip, covered with Blood.

October 17, 1993

UNTITLED (LINCOLN VS. KENNEDY)
||||||||||||||||||||||||||||||||||||||||||||||||

Think about this:

Abraham Lincoln was elected to Congress in 1846.
John F. Kennedy was elected to Congress in 1946.

Abraham Lincoln was elected president in 1860.
John F. Kennedy was elected president in 1960.

The names Lincoln and Kennedy each contain seven letters.

Both were particularly concerned with civil rights.

Both families lost a child while living in the White House.

Both presidents were shot on a Friday.

Both were shot in the head.

Here is an interesting one...

Lincoln's secretary was named Kennedy.
Kennedy's secretary was named Lincoln.

Both were assassinated by Southerners.
Both were succeeded by Southerners.

Both successors were named Johnson.

Andrew Johnson, who succeeded Lincoln, was born in 1808.
Lyndon Johnson, who succeeded Kennedy, was born in 1908.

John Wilkes Booth, who assassinated Lincoln, was born in 1839.
Lee Harvey Oswald, who assassinated Kennedy, was born in 1939.

Both assassins were known by their three names.

Both names comprise fifteen letters.

Booth ran from the theater and was caught in a warehouse.
Oswald ran from a warehouse and was caught in a theater.

Booth and Oswald were assassinated before their trials.

And last but not least...

A week before Lincoln was shot, he was in Monroe, Maryland.
A week before Kennedy was shot, he was in Marilyn Monroe.

THAT WHORE CALLED LIFE

||||||||||||||||||||||||||||||||||

"Do not go gentle into that good night."
Or so said a slightly more famous poet.
The grim reaper may eventually catch me.
But first, passionate sex with that whore called life.

Ah, to taste the juices of life.
Both men and women have their distinct flavors.
Even the saltiness of my blood.
Or a sweet cherry, which I plucked from "produce."
My tongue is a gateway to Earth.
I can lick the cream off an Oreo.
Or suck on a sour lemon drop.
Huevos rancheros and dim sum launch my tongue into orbit.

My big nose reminds me of brother Dog.
Most people have forgotten their canine ancestors.
To live is to take a big sniff of the world.
The musky dampness of my lover's underpants.
Vile McDonald's and the air of less fortunate animals.
Grease greets my nostrils.
My nose warns me of public restrooms.
Only the living can smell the dead.

Beautiful ears, bring me Beethoven,
As his ears could not.
The electric guitar of a man named Jimi
Penetrates my tympanic membrane.

The screeching and moaning of a lover.
The screeching and moaning of a car accident victim.
The sirens and gunshots of Inglewood.
The thief stole my ear, but I have another!

My big brown eyes select lovers with Darwinian accuracy,
As well as revealing where my naked body betrays me.
And, Mr. Huxley, I now can steal your words.
My pupils give me access to this "brave new world."

The wondrous human body,
If only it could roam the streets.
Clothes oppress my retinal fulfillment,
As tradition oppresses my mind.

The sense of touch.
My only excuse for living.
The wetness, the friction, the pressure
Of someone more than a friend.
The sharp of a broken finger bone.
My right arm reminded me of this four years straight.
Is there a line between pain and pleasure?
Sadomasochism is an art form.

All five senses in unison.
Is there a sixth?
An overwhelming rush of everything that is life.
One more day in the brothel called earth.
And one more night with that whore called life.

July 4, 1995

34

THE NIGHT BEFORE
THE OB-GYN EXAM (RADIO PLAYING)
||||||||||||||||||||||||||||||||||||||||||||||||||||

"Speak to me in a language I can feel."
Why does one feel most creative
When one most lacks the time for creativity?

"Make it last forever."
You may smash pumpkins,
But you will still grow bald.

"Let me out. Let me...let me out!"
I sat down on a sharp knife
That now tickles my stomach.

"Emptiness is loneliness
And loneliness is cleanliness
And cleanliness is godliness
And God is empty...just like ME."

Please slide to the edge of the table
And let your knees fall apart.
Now you feel my hand on your thigh.
Now for the electric screwdriver.

"Let's go for a ride."
Look in my big brown eyes.
Finally, it's starting to rhyme.
But when will you die?
Die, muthafucka, die!

We keep going, my blood still flowing.
You're still groaning and moaning.

If life is one big nightmare, wake me up...

(Quotes from the Smashing Pumpkins)

December 15, 1996

DIGWEED
|||||||||||

The disco ball drops down, and all we see are aliens and midget parts spewing over the dance floor. Intestines and blood. In the center, a traditional Iranian couple dances untraditionally. Actually, they're having sexual intercourse right in the center of the dance floor. Meanwhile, the intestines and blood drip down, along with the midget parts and aliens from the alien disco ball.

All the while, John Digweed plays a diabolical trance beat that is pure and primal, rich and tribal. As the sludge and grime drip off the people on the dance floor, intestines and midget body parts fall from the spherical dance ball disco world. And Digweed just keeps on playing. He just keeps on playing. And we just keep on dancing.

As long as I have one brain cell left, this night will never end.

September 2, 2004

THE PARTY
||||||||||||||

In the corner of a room lies
    the Truth.

The smoke from happy boys and girls
    rApes my lungs.

Freedom comes in the form of a pill
    with three letters.

Faces, so many faces, hover around me
    Like Social Vultures.

A story, a film, a play done one thousand times
    Over. And over, repeated perpetually.

An endless train of top 40 songs from the DJ
    Entertains us all,

Like a dog chasing his own
    Tail.

Desperate souls long to "hook up"

They will never be one with
    Themselves.

Outside, the air is COLD
My breath is white—
    Fresh Air and the Puff of a cigarette are
      One.

Tonight, the keg is God the wIsDumB
        From Hops.
Worth more than
Cold gold.

My old friend at my side,

Until the EMPTY chair next to
        Me
Is taken.

Shadows grow long.

Faces grow longer...

Father TIME grows longest of all...

March 1992

Happiness Is a Warm Pipe
IIIIIIIIIIIIIIIIIIIIIIIIIIIIIIIIIIIII

Pumpkins

"We only come out at night...
We only come out at night...
The daylight's much too bright..."

Boxing

Grab Holyfield's ear off the floor
And throw it back at the TV screen

CaN YoU fEeL Me?

Give me the Rock, you fiend.
See what I mean?
Let's get obscene.

I'm an Exhibitionist.
You're an Exhibitionist.
Voyeur, voyeur, I'm a submarine.

This is the back this and the the.

(Quote from the Smashing Pumpkins)

July 1997

STONED AND SOBER
||||||||||||||||||||||||||

My diary is important.
That's why my therapist has it.
If this is sauerkraut?

"When a man lies, he murders some part of this world.
These are the pale deaths men miscall their lives.
All this I cannot bear to stand.
Cannot the Kingdom of Salvation take me home?"

This song was written by a man in a shantytown outside of Johannesburg. A man who has lost faith in sauerkraut, while it boils and fails to support post-prandial flatulence and its request for economic sanctions against South Africa.

Am I Fucking You?

I'm Sorry.

I didn't mean to Fuck You.

Okedgeplaytheblues

You may see more clearly with your glasses on, but sometimes it's better not to see clearly.

December 1995

MANIMAL
||||||||||||

Ah the scent of a woman no the smell of a woman indeed as the lady passes by I close my eyes and take a deep breath through the nose first the perfume then deeper I smell her sweat her day's work under her armpits then deeper still I smell something more to the core I imagine myself with her my face buried between her legs this is the smell of a woman you may say I am a pervert but no when I am all in there smelling and doing everything that everyone wants to do I am real I am alive I am manimal.

February 17, 2001

ARE YOU HUNGARY?
||||||||||||||||||||||||||||

These places
Deep in the heart of Transylvania,
Whatever.
Red velvet lounges and black walls.
Unfortunately, we don't have forints.
Luscious, lovely ladies leer.
Even the score.

My two best friends,
Ultram and Jose Cuervo.
The flickering shadow of a candle.
In the mirror
We have no reflection.

Blood pulsing.
We must feed soon.
Sharpened teeth,
Saliva dripping,
We are hungry in Hungary?

Let's eat out Budapest.

May 19, 2004

CEREBRAL MASTURBATION
||||||||||||||||||||||||||||||||||||||

Can you create anything? You're tripped out on drugs that make you hot, drugs that make you wet, drugs that make you talk. You thrust deep into her asteroid. Oh my! This lullaby is not new. Screwing a dead old hooker on a Tijuana sidewalk. It gets old. Ramming, rrramming hot lllllincoln logs.

Porn cannot make poems. I'm searching for that empty feeling—you know, that one after your mom dies. But I've never felt so good. As I pause to write a very long sentence, the kind that makes you think of Dickens, I wonder if I bore into my own soul cell. I remember filming homemade porn where my colleague-director whipped it out and shot a load onto the set. Now, that was entertainment. This...This is just cerebral masturbation.

December 28, 2001

THE RIVER PHOENIX SHIT

IIIIIIIIIIIIIIIIIIIIIIIIIIIIIIIIII

NAIVE=EVIAN

I can't breathe!
Be me.
Be my crack fiend.
Please, please, please...

We, oh we
Shiny.
Don't turn your life
Upside down
Sharp guillotine
🚶☞🚶🚶✌☹

River Phoenix Shit

December 2004

THE IDIOT SAVANT
||||||||||||||||||||||||||

The Martians are coming! The Martians are coming!
With oval green heads and spaceships flying,
I surrender to their cosmic beam.
Erase my mind and begin again clean.
The FBI, the FBI, oh my, oh my, my.
Tapping my phone with a satellite in the sky.
You're not my mother! You're not my father!
You're just NYPD undercover!

I am the King of England, the Prince of Wales.
Bloody peasants, eat cake and get off my coattails.
I am powerful and rich, handsome and famous.
I freely commit crime, both trivial and heinous.

Marilyn Monroe, Madonna, and Janet Jackson,
They're all friends of mine, and you can just ask them.
Private parties and luxurious yachts,
Custom-made clothing and hydroponic pot.

-"Excuse me, Mr. President. It's time for your meeting, sir."
-"Uh, oh yes. I'll be right there. I was just collecting my
thoughts."

November 9, 1997

I'm Sick Again
||||||||||||||||||||

I'm sick of these foul henchmen of gloom
    Telling us that television is violent
        While they wage war on the sick and poor.

I'm sick of these video superchrists
    Telling us to rebel against the system
        While they milk every drop from the system.

I'm sick of the pseudo-biology students
    Spending every day inside with a textbook
        While trees wonder where their brethren went.

I'm sick of this war against drugs,
    Telling the children marijuana is evil,
        While the government dumps cocaine onto the
        streets.

I'm sick of idiots.

I'm sick of college "student" athletes
    Reinforcing stereotypes
        By blowing snot onto the sidewalk.

I'm sick of these sellout radio stations
    Playing forty minutes of commercials
        And twenty minutes of the same three songs.

I'm sick of the games men and women play.
It's really quite simple.
Talk?

I'm sick of being sick,
Spreading the seed of my incurable disease,
The human brain.

December 1993

HEROIN
||||||||||

"It's my wife
It's my life"
As Velvet Underground
Put it down
But now

Art is not for the oblivious
It's ridiculous
Idiot.

H
Smack
Dope
"I'm a creep."
"Your skin makes me cry."

Duragesic patch
Fentanyl
MS Contin
Vicodin, Percocet, lortab, hydrocodone, oxycontin,
Oxycodone, codeine, Demerol, dilaudid, buprenorphine
Methadone.

"If I die tonight."
"Lord Knows"

Lord doesn't know.
No one knows.
Have the balls to admit it,
Kid.

Quick! Give him Narcan.
He's dead.

October 22, 2004

One Sentence
||||||||||||||||||||||

At the end of your day, when all your words have failed and your friends have gone home, you wash your face, look in the mirror, and realize your explicit and overt denial of what is cliché will ultimately be, simultaneously, your worst downfall and greatest triumph.

October 2004

BRAINSTORM
||||||||||||||||

Sometimes the slippery seashells at my feet give way and I feel as though my thoughts are sometimes the slippery seashells at my feet give way and I feel as though my thoughts are confused.

Break with haste. I'm sick of it. What else? The hens, the peckers—you know, silently sitting by the seashore. You find this therapeutic, do you? Fuck you. See. This opera, this island, this firmament. My mind is a toad. Stirring up these thickets will cause the most foul odor. Sinking, sinking, stinking, stinking. I'm an excellent driver. Doctor, what do you mean I have a brain lesion? Chaos—what y'all know about chaos? I am a big boy.

It's just not happening today. Sometimes you have good sometimes you have good days.

May 31, 1995

LA CAVE *2003*
IIIIIIIIIIIIIIIIIIII

Listen, have you ever felt like you're a Martian?
Insatiable, more is not enough.
Fuck jazz in the worst way,
Rectally with no Vaseline.

Give me a trance beat six hours straight.
A bottle of E.
Put my tongue in a sling when I'm done.

Silly, silly, silly
Lum, lum, chichichichacha
Fuck the igpay atinlay
I'm razycay
In the worst way...

Can you feel your blood pumping?

May 2004

APARTMENT 304
||||||||||||||||||||||

Trapped in my cell...
With the trappings of a cell.
Behold, my skin is not yet cold.
I grow old; I grow old.

I am free to leave
But I have nowhere to be.
There must be mold
On the window of my soul.

Crabgrass grows on my heart.
In this play called life, I have no part.
A call on the phone.
Mister, please leave me alone.

Quicksand isn't quick enough.
Thoughts of death only wake me up.
I must get out. I must roam.
So, so very tired of being alone.

Step up, step out, step off,
My friends, this train is lost!
Isolate the madman
So he can kill all that he can.

Sleepy, to sleep and sleep
Into the dark and dangerous deep.
But why? Try to understand.
This college man has done all that he can.

August 27, 1993

HELLISH INTOLERABLE VIOLENCE

Until we meet again,
My friends

See how it kills my friends,
We're dead.

You!
Hangman.

I know that the world is slow.
I know that the World is slow!

A...I...D...S...
Any ideas?

July 1994

CONFESSIONS OF A TERRORIST
||||||||||||||||||||||||||||||||||||||||||

"Hi, everyone. This is your stoned temple pilot speaking. Currently, we are sixty-nine thousand feet high and flying higher even still. I would like to personally thank each and every one of you for choosing Percocet Airlines. Here at Percocet, we don't just get you there on time, we also get you there high."

The captain droned on and on, but I couldn't pay attention. Everything was so warm and cozy now. I was a chunk of butter, melting slowly on a frying pan. My muscles and bones endured a process of liquefaction, transforming me into nothing more than giggles. Roughly one hour had passed since I had washed down the magical pills with a glass of Tanqueray and tonic.

As I looked out the window, I once again saw my old friends, the big, puffy white clouds. We had met when I was just a wee-bit child. On perhaps every plane trip I had ever been on, when I was fortunate enough to have a window seat, I would glue my face to the window and imagine flying within the clouds. I would imagine floating in and out, up and down, through and through these great condensations of humidified air.

Now, as an a-dull-t, much had changed. Sure, I was high. Sure I had to be responsible. But, nevertheless, I was back to the carefree days of youth. Did it really matter how I got there, as long as I got there? The only thing different now was the sex. Through my headphones purred on the sounds of Montell Jordan's "Get it on Tonight," and all I could think about was groping this girl next to me. I don't believe that this feeling between my legs had been there when I was eight years old.

"Ladies and gentlemen, this is your stoned temple pilot again. We are now flying over New York City. Those of you on the left side of the plane will get a good view of the World Trade Center. Those of you on the right will get a good view of the big, puffy white clouds..."

My buzz had completely worn off, and I had found myself waking up from a short nap. Drool and snot webs had run from my nose onto the plane window. Out of the corner of my eye, I could see the girl sitting next to me, peering at me with disgust.

The time had come for me to take care of my intended business. I reached under the seat and grabbed my back-pack. I kissed my Allah necklace, stood up, and made my announcement.

"Ladies and gentlemen, Allahu Akbar, this is a hijacking. In this backpack, I have a bomb, and I will not hesitate to blow all of you muthafuckas up unless you do exactly as I say."

My announcement was not received as calmly as I had antic-ipated. Everyone began screaming. The passengers seated near me tried to move back. The girl next to me started crying and tucked her head between her legs. I moved my way into the aisle and withdrew my snub-nose .22 caliber handgun, which had so conveniently traveled within the hollowed-out interior of my cell phone.

One of the flight attendant guys rushed down the aisle toward me with a bigger gun, screaming, "Drop that gun! Drop that gun!"

As I was no longer in the mood to converse, I let off three rounds into his head. Brain matter splattered everywhere. One of the bullets punctured a hole through the plane. The cabin began to lose pressure as the oxygen masks dropped down.

Well, I had done my job. This distraction had enabled my colleagues to gain entry into the cockpit, smoke the stoned temple pilot, and change the course of the plane. The last thing I remember, as I blew a kiss to the big, puffy white clouds, was looking at the building approaching and seeing a little girl eating brunch at Windows on the World. Then we all became high-speed dirt.

September 11, 2001

BUDAPEST WORLD TOUR 2004
|||||||||||||||||||||||||||||||||||||||||||||

This town is fucked. Searched three hours to find breakfast at McDonald's. Can't exchange thousands in euros or dollars for a fucking forint. No one speaks English, not even the tourists. Treated like a goddamn stepchild...

MURDERER
||||||||||||||

    I am a murderer. I know it sounds crazy, but the first time I killed someone, it felt like losing my virginity. I was stress-free and relaxed after I did it. More worldly. More experienced. I wouldn't go so far as to say I'm a serial killer. I've only killed three times, and I probably won't kill again.

    You think this story is a joke, but think again. Until you have actually taken another human life, you are missing out on the fun. It's just as I said. Imagine trying to explain the feeling of sex to a virgin. Imagine trying to explain an acid trip to someone who has never tried drugs.

    Actually, I'm behind you right now. Hmm...Maybe one more time.

September 12, 2004

THE RAVING MADMAN
||||||||||||||||||||||||||||||

Pure shit.
That's how I feel every day,
Not once a week, not once a month.
Every day.

Pure shit.
No matter what I do, I cannot escape.
My mind runs wild,
Throwing me into the well of manure.

I long to giggle and fart,
To dance on the gardenous beach with monkeys.
Oh, how I wish I could juggle.
What large teeth you have, my dear.

Rolling, rumbling, rambling—save.
Trapping, tripping, tricking—me.
Mauling, milking, molesting—from.
Petting, pawing, pouring—me.

Deep shit.
The vapors enter my nostrils.
This sewer finds its way to my brain.
Every day.

Deep shit.
Hot and warm, smothers my face.
Wet and sticky, stuck in my hair.
I bathe my body in urine.

Bowling for dollars,
Feel my brain crack like an egg.
Its juice seeps out
Onto your newly waxed tile floor.

My girl sleeps with my best friend.
Wrong, not sleep—fuck.
My girl is fucking my best friend.
Seven slippery seals sat sunning silently on the seashore.

Me, I am the night.
I probe in and out of love like a searchlight.
I have always lived alone and will die alone.
Of course, I enjoy eating cheese.

Just say, "I love you."
She would not.
I raped her violently on the floor of one forest path.
My demon seed found its way through her forest path.

She was supposed to love it.
She did not love it.
She hated it.
I hated it more.

Hey, little boy, want some candy?
I molested him with my phallic thumb of love.
He loved it.
I loved it more.

The cow and the yodeler are one.
Help, somebody, please help me!
The cow and the yodeler are one.
The cow—help!—and the yodeler—please!—are one.

The cow had the yodeler for lunch.

June 7, 1994

IRANIAN DOCTOR, GERMAN CAR, AMERICAN VALUES
||||||||||||||||||||||||||||

The engineers of luxury have offered a driving experience that is steeped in tradition, yet utterly distinctive and unique. Turn the key, and the engine comes to life, charging to reach 62 miles per hour in just 6.4 seconds. The maximum speed is a remarkable 157 miles per hour. Lightweight materials are used to maximize stability and improve response. Straight-line performance is smooth and consistent, as is high-speed, mid-corner handling. Above all, however, the most important feature is the car's singular perfection on the road. A Porsche Boxster is much more than an expertly engineered sports car. It's an experience—one that transcends the cars and the years to stir the souls of enthusiasts everywhere, bringing them together as a family. For the most part, this so-called family of owners tends to have much in common. Eager to move up the ladder to a higher distinction of social class, their purchase of such a car that embodies masculinity, success, and economic status allows them agency to express their own sense of identity and, at the same time, a form of culture.

I can analyze firsthand the importance of this particular make of car as an expression of its owner, for I know my brother too well. According to Ben, the basis of his relationship with his car is formed by a very personal interpretation of the word *freedom*. My brother Ben is a single thirty-one-year-old medical doctor. He dreamed of buying a Porsche when he was living and working hard as a resident in the bustling and swarming city of New York, where getting from one place to another in a cab is difficult enough. Of course, he envisioned the Porsche as part of a lifestyle that he wanted to create for himself when he moved back to Southern California. He predicted that, once he became a doctor, the fast car that is deemed much better than others in its class would pave a clear path to fast women and fast music. As he now reaps the benefits of life as a physician and remembers being a struggling student in the distant past, never in his life has he felt freer than he does today. Having finally bought the ideal condominium just five blocks from the beach in Los Angeles, Ben does not live alone, for surely the company of his Porsche does as much for him as he does for it.

He purchased the small silver two-seater convertible two years ago before he was able to buy his own place and when he was still living with our dad and grandmother. Able to do whatever he wanted all throughout college, medical school, and residency in New York City, the transition to living under the same roof with family proved to be difficult, as his personal space and private life were constantly interfered with. It was during this time in which Ben bought his car, his symbol of independence, freedom, and success. Our father was initially outraged at what he believed to be an imprac-tical economical decision on his son's part. He attempted to persuade Ben that buying a Porsche simply did not make sense at the time, or maybe ever. Although, one must remember that symbols do not make sense if they are not yours. As they often appear in times of change or turmoil, symbols have the ability to control and stabilize those times, and that is precisely what the Porsche did for Ben two years ago. It is important to elaborate on the origin of our father's traditional views because, although Ben was born in Iran, it was only a year later that he and my family moved to the United States, where they have resided ever since. Our father's strong objection to the Porsche was most likely due to the fact that he could not identify with the American values it epitomized, while my brother, who was raised here, easily could. Unable to fully control how my brother spent his own money, our father could only convince him to buy the less expensive Boxster model as opposed to the costly Carrera. Fifty thousand dollars later, Ben was able to take control and differentiate himself from who he was with who he had become "as opposed to the shapeless mass of the many, (high culture) helps the elite to recognize themselves and one another in the drab mass of society and to learn their mission which consists in being few and holding their own against the many...Like the culture industries it defines itself against, modernist high culture owes its very existence to the success of the capitalist market economy." As Ben eventually moved into his own place away from home, his Porsche took on a more social and specific meaning. He finally began to live out the image of himself that he had foreseen for a long time without any constraints, that which he simply could not do with Dad and Grandma around. His car, he claims, is merely "training wheels for sports cars," as he one day hopes to buy what he truly has always wanted—a Ferrari. The only circumstance where he would consider keeping the Porsche is if it continues to be state of the art. If it is not, he will surely sell it, as he refuses to drive "an old man's car."

In the meantime, Ben continues to invest quite a bit of time, money, and energy into the object of his freedom, fast life, and bachelorhood. When he initially bought the car, he made it uniquely his, installing a new sound system, changing the headlights to clear ones, getting eighteen-inch rims, getting turbo-style rims, installing a stability-management system, painting the word PORSCHE onto the spoiler, adding a barbed-wire-style license plate holder, and getting a personalized license plate. He also plans on installing a rear cabinet, which serves as a shelf for storage space as well as two additional speakers. The reality is that the car is better kept than it is showcased. Ben avoids parking outdoors as much as he can, but when he does, he is sure to distance it from other cars. Even in the most posh neighborhoods, he always attaches the bar lock to his steering wheel, just in case. Not even the valet companies are permitted to drive Ben's Porsche, seeing as though he usually parks the car right up front so he can see it from the window of the restaurant where he is having dinner. In fact, one time, they moved it without his permission and dented his car. Fortunately, the valet company paid for it.

Since then, he always keeps the key safe in his pocket and gets routine custom details to maintain both its inward and outward cleanliness. Ben gets particularly agitated when a passenger of his eats in the car or enters with sandy feet. His passengers simply cannot understand why it matters so much to him, but they can see that it clearly does. With a car of that caliber, it is easy to see why he drives fast and with the top down. Not only does it give him a sense of control over the road, but of the police as well. Multiple times, he has been pulled over, but so far, he has been able to escape a ticket, as he often legitimately claims he is on the way to see a patient. The fact that Ben continually pays immense attention to his Porsche confirms the importance of the car to him, while it serves him daily by giving him his own form of self-representation. We express who we are through our possessions, especially those that are the most valuable to us. The Porsche is Ben's expression of pop culture because it not only has relevancy, but also significant value to him, as it sustains and maintains his identity. For Ben, the Porsche once gave him an American sense of identity that was culturally different from those of his parents, as it represented manhood, independence, and accomplishment. One could say that Ben's Porsche within American culture has almost a playboy connotation to it, as there is only room for one other passenger. The car has become symbolic, maintaining that status for him, as meaningful objects that surround us give us our own form of self-representation. The bachelor pad completed the image of himself that he had envisioned so long ago. "Although the world certainly exists in all its enabling and constraining materiality outside representation, it is only in practices of representation that the world can be made to mean. Representation constructs the reality it appears only to describe." Living the bachelor lifestyle makes the Porsche all the more important to Ben, as it solidifies that particular status. The more he personalizes the vehicle, the more it becomes a part of him. The essence of culture is what one has created and its direct relationship to what one becomes. Ben does not identify with any Porsche. It is his own that he values so much; it is a controlled area over which he has complete authority. Others might only see the monetary value of his prized possession, when, in fact, it means so much more to him. "We are classified by our classifications and classify others by theirs." He consumes it as a means of control that enables him to remake culture in his own terms. It will never stop seizing to represent, shape, and create his American values of being forever young, single, and part of a higher social class.

S.Z., 2002

BULLETS ARE HOT
||||||||||||||||||||||||||||

Oh my god, I've been shot.
All alone, left to die.
Your misery is that I'm gonna live.
And when I find you, bye-bye.
Bullets are hot, burning.
Fuck you, I'm gonna take your life.

Ahhh! You want a War. I'll wage your fucking war.
Ahhh! You want a War. I'll wage your fucking WAR!

ON THE EDGE OF A ROOF
||||||||||||||||||||||||||||||||||

Welcome to planet Earth.
It used to be true, but it's lost its worth.

See them kill each other.
Father Time grows old, gone Earth our mother.

Run away from this painful place.
Helpless and hopeless, they are a disgrace.

Take my life, don't watch the kids die.
Don't turn me away, find truth in my eyes.

Deceiver—stop your life and I'll let you in.
Killer—drop your knife, you'll lose in the end.

Joker—laugh your laughs and I'll take you down.
Roamer—stay with me, I'll turn you around.

Protector—tell us all what this is about.
Cheater—no hope for you, I'll knock you out.

These are the times I've so waited for
When men are men, like I've seen before.
With women—no games, don't act like whores.
Don't look away 'cause he's old and poor.

These are the times I've so waited for
When acting and faking goes out the door.
So she gives her all, but I want more.
But what the hell am I looking for?

Useless

Aimless

The helpless and the hopeless.

1989

KILL THE RADICAL
||||||||||||||||||||||||

Sometimes, when I'm writing poetry like this, I think to myself, *Goddamn, I'm a hard muthafucka.* But then sometimes I'll feel all warm and bubbly inside, and I'll want to pet animals 'n shit.

Let me give you an example. Just the other day, while I was walking down the street, I ran into this guy walking his horse. He said he was taking his horse to the movies.

I said, "What! What the fuck you talkin' about, Jack? You gonna tell me that you're takin' your muthafuckin' horse to the movies? To the muthafuckin' cinema!"

"That's right," he said.

"You can't take no horse to the theater."

"And why not?"

"Because that's the way it is. You can't take no horse to the movies. These theaters are for people. Humans, muthafucka. Where the fuck you from? Iowa or fuckin' India 'n shit?"

"I understand the rules and regulations of our modern society, mister. But let me tell you that my horse is dandy. This is not your average horse you see on the streets. Daisy's the most beautiful horse in all the world. Why, just look at her!"

I looked this muthafucka straight in the eye, and I knew he musta been trippin'. Crack-smoking muthafucka. But then I looked at his horse. And you know what? It kinda did look nice. Then I thought I was trippin', so I rubbed my eyes, stepped back, and took another look. Jesus H. Christ. When I looked again, I just couldn't believe it. This had to be the most beautiful horse in the world. In fact, it was the most beautiful creature I had ever seen. It was even more beautiful than the best women on earth.

But then I thought, *What the fuck am I talkin' about? I'm talking about a fuckin' horse. Fuckin' I must be the one smokin' the crack.* But then I looked at it again, and it was even more beautiful. Man, I can't even describe it! It had smooth hair and a pretty soft-brown color and big, innocent brown eyes.

So I said to the man, "Yo, you know you really do have a fine-lookin' horse. Now I guess I can see why you're takin' your horse out on the town and all."

"Why, thank you very much," replied the man. "I take great pride in Daisy, and I only take her to the finest restaurants and motion pictures that money can buy. Then she takes care of me as well."

"You are one lucky son of a bitch," I told him. "If other guys could..." I paused. *What the fuck? Wait a minute!* I rubbed my eyes again, took another step back, and noticed for the first time that this muthafuckin' dude was buck naked.

"Yo, man, you got no muthafuckin' clothes on!"

"That's right, I always travel in the nude when I take Daisy to the theater."

Aw, I'd had enough of this shit. I reached into my coat and pulled out my snub-nosed .357 Magnum. I clicked off the safety and let off three caps into this dude's chest.

Without even flinching, he looked at me and said, "You can't kill me. I am only a mere product of the hallucination caused by your carotid thrombosis."

"All right, then." So I put the gun to my own head, closed my eyes, and pulled the trigger. Nothing happened. So I did it again. Still, nothing happened. I kept firing while the man started laughing. Then the horse started laughing. They both were laughing. They laughed so loud that other people on the street stopped to see what was going on. When the other people saw what I was doing, they started laughing, too. Pretty soon, I had a big fuckin' crowd around me, all laughin' while I tried to kill myself.

After a while, the laughter started to echo more and more. Then it started to fade away, along with all the people, until everything just started to float away. My thoughts started to get fuzzy and abstruse. I was beginning to get the idea that maybe someone had drugged me somehow. Damn! Was I caught slippin'? One minute, I felt like a hard muthafucka; the next, I felt all warm and bubbly inside. But it's all good. Because I started getting real, real dizzy. At first, I was kinda scared, but then it felt kinda good, kinda cozy, kinda warm and bubbly. Then, slowly, life itself SLIPPED AWAY, and all was dark.

July 9, 1995

WHAT I BELIEVE IN
||||||||||||||||||||||||||

#1: I believe in life. To be alive includes the sensations of touch, taste, smell, sight, and hearing. I greatly value all of these senses. To be deprived of any one of these senses would mean being deprived of a part of life. I would consider death to be the permanent removal of these five senses and, also, of thought and breath. Whatever happens after death is questionable. I will leave that topic for philosophers and evangelists. For my purposes, I consider life better than death. So I would like to enjoy being alive until I reach the point where I feel death is permanently better than life.

#2: I respect the lives of others. I do not expect everyone to value their life the way in which I value mine, but I do believe that everyone should have the freedom to decide what they want to do with their lives. "Live and let live" is a good rule. I would like to love with this motto in mind. As for those who do not follow this motto and attempt to interfere negatively with the life of another, I would hope they would be removed from society. I do not support the idea of taking the lives of others under any circumstances, unless my life or the lives of others is in danger. "Fight fire with fire" is a ridiculous motto. From my experiences, I have learned that water does a much better job of putting out a fire.

April 29, 1992

Hard-Boiled
||||||||||||||||||

the young boy walks hard along the road
no sights, no sounds, no lights of reality exist here
empty space where a smile once dent

soon the dark comes to lighten the load
endless walk, pointless path, straightly talk, and yet not so near
echoes ring of a time well spent

noise breaks the serenity's abode
a car, black yet white, with flashing lights pulls up to this rear
the boy withdraws food quick from lent

death comes ripping hard along the road
end of a time, end of the line, the lad exists not here
quick draw from a quick pig, all was meant

dO nOt AtTeMpT tO wItHdRaW yOuR eGgS fRoM tHe CaSe

March 12, 1991

The Mother I Never Knew
||||||||||||||||||||||||||||||||||||||||||

She's a slutty little wench with a red, raw three-inch clitoris and bulging vaginal lips. Cavernous pussy. Red, rotten, and too ripe. You would never believe she also had a perfect ass with a sphincter so tight it brought back the memories of a true anal void. Drip, drip, drip...The drops would drop off her opening like dew, only stickier and greener. Sticky. Green. Mmmm...Sounds delish. Oh no! A severed dick just popped out of her pussy. I guess I now know why her pussy was bulging red. I guess I should...Wait! Where's my penis? It's in her twat. But soon, it will be in the garbage disposal. She will grind it to a pulp in garlic and sesame oil—bitch!

Why do I suddenly crave sausage pizza? I need to take back my dick, should I ever hope to live again. But first, let me have some french fries since I'm a bit hungry. Ah, yes indeed! These french fries hit the spot, all right! But that last one tasted a bit strange. Yow! I done just blasted off. Can't feel my head. Can't feel my...my nose! The last fry was my nose. Fuck! What will I sniff pussy with? This bitch wants to take it all. Time to whack this cunt. Where's that blasted .44 Magnum at? I must have left it in my pants in the bathroom. Let's see, if I can just find it...Rats! It's gone. But what's this? A gateway to a new dimension. "Agamemnon!" But before we go, I just found my Swiss army knife. Time to corkscrew this bitch through the skull. Pull out some brains when we're finished, too. She's a dead, lifeless mass now. Now I can live in peace.

The mother I never knew.

THE PEEPER
||||||||||||||

Hey, girl alone.
No need to fix your bed today.
Your clean sheets are hardly astray.
Your wild oats sewn?
Big, plump, and round,
The ugly fat girl of the block.
Your king-sized bed broke from the shock.
Sad circus clown.

Large clear window
With no curtains, take a look out.
My balcony's how I find out
When you're home.

Yes, I saw you
Naked, running around the room.
My new camera with auto-zoom,
You never knew.

All the kids laughed.
Big mistake, your trip to the beach.
"Beached whale! Is the harpoon in reach?"
Mad? Glad you left?
I'm so sorry.

It's humankind's nature to be cruel.
Yes, we are savage, stupid fools.
But I still watch.
Because I...I am the peeper.

September 1993

ORCHIDE
||||||||||

When out, my deaf soul cannot hear the screams of this loud emptiness. This, in turn, leads to dining and merriment at a more blissful level, unencumbered by the weight—the sheer weight of all your bullshit.

On the flip side of this stamp, Iranian culture does not stop at 2:00 a.m. We have a certain stickiness. Sticky greens and sticky floors. Lapping up cow brains, we peer at the girls sweating it out on the dance floor. We have done this for a thousand years.

September 6, 2004

FANTASY PLANET
||||||||||||||||||||||||

Alive, I'm gripping, I'm fighting to be
Life, a vivid orb through the
Black, to touch the soil, to feel the
Flesh, as I decay I'd like to know what's
Real, hot interlocked hands or just a vow of
Love, before I was born I was already
Dead, ah, to see the news, watch the gunman
Kill, we dwell like pigs as we swim in our
Shit

Heat, the giver of life taunts our
Time, and urgency a frantic rush to
Be, be where I've been, what it's like to be
Cold, just a frigid kick and here comes the
Dark, an endless pit into which we all must
Fall, and four tears I've cried and for tears I'll
Die, one more death on the news, so
What, we dwell like pigs as we swim in our
Shit

Screeeeeams!
Tonight, I laugh as the jungle takes us
All, oh, don't be sad for me 'cause I've lost my
Mind, I'm reaching out for the one they call
God, I know she'd help me if I had enough

Faith, tell a tale, tell me more soothful
Lies, now it's got hold, it's time for me to go
Down, I've drowned like the pigs, just a part of the
Shit

1989

OF SPICS AND SPADES

IIIIIIIIIIIIIIIIIIIIIIIIIIIIIII

Who am I to hate someone just for the color of one's skin?
Who am I to judge someone without even knowing who she is?
All I've found in this world is hatred and bigotry.
Can't let my kids go through life with this same type of misery.

Come to hell with me.
One shot from my gun.
Not as good as me,
Should we be as one?

I'm better than you.
Hatred in my soul,
I know that it's true.
That's what I've been told.

Kill that man with an iron fist.
Take his life like the rest.
Find his home and run down his child.
Rape his wife, they are so wild.

Ignorance is nothing new.
Tell me who are the chosen few.
"Spics" and "spades," such foolish words
Fight for the weak, they shall be heard.

Anger builds up in me, I can't respect such racist pigs.
Taken my home and my family, I think it's time for you to pay.
People talk about fixing this world, ending war, and gaining peace.
Take a look, it begins right here, we are all brothers, so what's to fear?

As I look to the sky, I really wonder who's way up high.
Would a god make such a place where man kills, where man kills?
They say, "Get the hell out, get the hell back to that place you call your home."
I say, "Look around. Safety in numbers. Don't let me find you when you're alone."

1990

THE COLLABORATION
||||||||||||||||||||||||||||

One day, while yachting in the Caribbean,
A cold tadpole of a boy wet his underpants.

Time passes without compromise, shedding
Upon us the debris of unfinished journeys.

Oh, hark the pale yell of the minstrel!
Oh, minstrel yell of the pale hark!

Our fingers linger in tunnels
Of humid, dark fluid-filled chambers
     Where bubbly pale secretions abound.
     With pheromones.
Hear the joy of the juices as we plunge deeper.

A large liMoUsine is parked snugly in the GARAge—
With the sole purpose of creating a mirage,
Until we drift high up into the clouds, only to return ever so gently
To this mud hole called Earth, where I wish I drove a Bentley.

Deception is one among many branches generated by...
My nerve cells, for I am unable to possess K+ in my body.

The reality of existence is the existence of reality.

April 1994

THE COLLABORATION II
||||||||||||||||||||||||||||||||

The masses await with humbled arms outstretched
To massively bring down wretched
An event, ever so enthusiastically far-fetched.
The gleeful crowd enters the big top,
Only to find they were part of the ring pot.
        Definition
            Definition
                Definition
                    Definition

Anyways, I was out to get laid
And then I laid an egg and was paid.
Paid was laid I, when laid got you
Paid and laid, ventured to Penny Lane tried and true.

Stoned!
Are you?
If I were you and you were me, then we would see jointly.
Jazz!
Zzaj!
Coolest of the cool, don't drool you fool, ya might get schooled.

A master clocksman with tools
That sets into motion the mechanism that runs all the fools.
Fools with rules, by the tools created schools spawning fools
and rules.
      Rules rule all—borders abound.

The reality of existence is the existence of reality.

May 1994

In gOD We Trust
||||||||||||||||||||||||||||||

Well, here we are.
This is our campus, our city, our world.
Yeah, we have plenty of problems these days, and we also have many people out there who think they have the answers.

What is the answer?
Who out there thinks he has the answer?
Well, maybe you do. Maybe you don't.

Here's a suggestion:
What about believing in gOD?
That's right—what about believing in gOD and all the ways that gOD can help us?

Maybe we should look to gOD for love and guidance.
After all, people with this love for gOD came to America to escape religious persecution.

Yes, these were the same people who spread this love of gOD to the many Native Americans of this continent.

Any Native Americans out there?
Maybe a few. There could be more, but we all know what happened to the Native Americans.
In case you don't know, let me tell you.
These gOD-loving people, under the guise of "manifest destiny," killed them.
Not just the young men. But the women and children. The sick and the old.

Oh, but they weren't all killed.
Some lived and were put on reservations, where many still live today.

But wasn't it nice of these gOD-loving people to put the last few remnants of the American Indians onto reservations? A free home—how bad is that?
Do any of you live next door to the largest nuclear testing and dumping sites in this country?
The Native Americans do.

Some people may say, "Hey, it's the government's fault the Native Americans were massacred."
"It wasn't the fault of God or the people who love God."

Well, to these people, I say, "Take a look at a penny, or a nickel, or a quarter, or a dollar bill, or any other form of US currency. For those of you who can't read, it says, 'In God We Trust.' What you have learned in your history class is wrong. There is no separation between church and state. They are one and the same."

Every kid who has been raised in a public school in this country has said the Pledge of Allegiance at least a thousand times. The Pledge of Allegiance states that we are "one nation, under God."
Well, if the government trusts gOD, then so should I, right?
If we love gOD enough, we don't need to love our own brothers and sisters.
This is the type of logic that leads to three hundred years of slavery.
Yes, the gOD-loving people who murdered all the Native Americans are the same gOD-loving people who murdered

over one hundred million Africans and enchained them like dogs for three hundred years.

I, too, would want gOD on my side if I were going to cold-bloodedly kill innocent men and hot-bloodedly rape innocent women.
The Native Americans have the reservation.
The African Americans have the ghetto.
You can thank gOD for that.

The biggest problem in this country isn't drugs. It isn't AIDS. It isn't poverty.
The biggest problem in this country is religion.

Fuck religion!
I hope at least I have the freedom to fuck religion if I want to.

And while I'm at it, I'd also like to fuck gOD, fuck Jesus Christ, fuck Allah, fuck Mohammed, fuck Buddha, and fuck any other so-called deities and their prophets.

And if I offended anyone today, my apologies.
But maybe you need to be offended.
I think we'd all be much closer to solving the problems on this planet if we loved our fellow human beings as much as we love our religious idols.

Love each other first.

July 29, 1992

NEW YORK
||||||||||||||||||||||||||||||||||||

I Like Smoking Crack
||||||||||||||||||||||||||||||||

She takes the empty can of soda and crumples it up a bit, forming a little bowl. She then takes a needle and pokes about ten holes into the base of this bowl. She lights a cigarette and taps the ash over these holes, forming a cozy little nest. This is the crack pipe.

She takes some of the off-white crack powder and places it in the nest. She moves the flame of a lighter over the powder while he places his lips over the drinking pout of the can and inhales deeply. He moves away from the can and blows out the smoke—light, sweet, metallic smoke. Crack smoke. At first, he feels nothing, but then, one minute later, it starts to hit him. And then, before he can utter a word...blick... blick...*BLAUW! How do you like me now?*

"I see death around the corner. Tryin' to stay high while I survive in the city where the skinny niggaz die!" J blurted out.

"J, what are you talking about?" asked Pac as he released another cloud of crack smoke.

"I'm talking about this. We're fucking smoking crack!"

"J, you're too uptight," interjected Cat as she loaded up yet another powdery bowl of crack. She then passed the can over to T-dog, who at that moment had the expression of someone who really believed he had just made first contact with space aliens. He had this huge ear-to-ear grin, and his eyes were half-open but completely rolled back, like they were examining the current damage to his brain.

"So, T-dog, how are you enjoying your first crack experience?" J earnestly asked.

"It's cool," T-dog said. But then he moved closer to J and whispered, *"But it'd be better if I could fuck Cat."*

"Take it easy, T-dog. Don't you know? Everyone has their roles to play," J retorted.

And so the four crack smokers smoked and smoked some more. They proceeded to get higher and higher, while also redefining the common stereotype of a crack fiend. Here they were. All college graduates—three doctors and one schoolteacher. One Korean, one Indian, one Persian, and one Jew.

"Hey, Pac," J said. "You know that place between your ears where the bird's nest and the cobwebs are, the place where your brain should be...?"

"Fuck you, J."

Everyone giggled.

J grinned. "What would your mother say?" he asked.

"You're a goddamn boo boo," Pac answered.

"Boo boo, boo boo! What the fuck is that shit? Boo boo. Is that the best you can come up with?" J taunted.

"All right, then," Pac tried again. "You goddamn camel jockey muthafucka."

"Camel jockey? Who you callin' camel jockey, you curry-smellin' coconut juggler?"

"Fuck you, you hairy Middle Eastern sand nigga!"

"Fuck you, you elephant-riding, turban-wearing, dot-on-the-forehead darkie."

"I've had enough of this, you sweaty, hair-on-your-back towel head." And with that, Pac grabbed J by the arm and threw him on the floor. The two began to wrestle, knocking over everything in their path. They moved their way through the living room, flipping over the coffee table, knocking over the standing floor lamp, stepping on the dog, and basically, just making a big mess of the tiny Brooklyn apartment. T-dog made a feeble attempt to stop them, but his intoxication proved to be the determining factor, as he tripped over his own feet and fell facedown on the floor.

Cat sprang from the couch and tackled J and Pac. The three of them fell onto the bed and continued wrestling.

"Hey, no pinching!" J shouted as he recoiled from Cat's pinch to his thigh. He retaliated by grabbing one of her breasts and twisting it.

"Hey, that hurts, and no titty-twisting."

"Leave her alone, you brute," added Pac as he pushed J away and sat on Cat, who had been lying on her back. Without another word, Pac kissed Cat on the lips—once. She then grabbed the back of his head and pulled him toward her, and they kissed again. This time they didn't stop. Mouths open, tongues dancing, they continued to enjoy their crack high at this new and exciting level.

Cat moaned in delight. Pac looked down and noticed that, while he had been busy kissing Cat, J had taken off her pants and had relocated his mouth between her legs. Pac continued to kiss Cat while moving his hands to cup her small but eager breasts. J also began to use his hands, probing a finger in and out of her deep recess while continuing to slurp and munch, munch and slurp.

Not surprisingly, Cat began to buck her hips uncontrollably and let out a little yelp. All the commotion aroused T-dog from the floor and into a seated position from which he observed the three mattress frolickers with a mild, intoxicated disbelief.

Yet, the three were undaunted by this one-man audience and continued onward. Cat had managed to disrobe both men in her frenzy and was now preparing to be mounted. She assumed "the position" on her hands and knees and bobbed her head forward, capturing Pac's item in her mouth like a circus sword-swallower. At the same time, J attacked from the rear, entering her in true canine form. They all began to thrust and plunge in unison. The three maintained a steady course in this manner for roughly half an hour. They transformed the classic image of Shakespeare's "beast with two backs" into a more contemporary "gyrating centipede with six legs."

Perhaps motivated by sheer lust or simply impending orgasm, J decided to give Cat the proverbial slap on the ass. He raised his arm up and, with fingers outstretched, came down with all his might on Cat's right buttock. *Pow!*

"*Owwww!*" Cat screamed as she recoiled from the two men.

Pac was laughing hysterically.

"*Why'd you hit me?*"

"*What? I didn't hit you; I slapped you on the ass. You were supposed to like it.*"

"*Like it? That hurt. I didn't like that shit at all!*"

"*Yeah well, it had to be...It makes things more interesting, anyway. Your thighs are like butter, easy to spread. Besides, I'm starting to sober up.*"

"*J,*" Pac interjected, "*you fucked everything up, but... That shit was hella funny. Aw, come on, Cat...It's all good.*" And with that, Pac moved over to Cat and started kissing her feet. He moved slowly up to her ankles, combining his kisses with brief interludes of lashings from his tongue. He reached her knees, and her legs slowly parted, giving him a glimpse of the adventure that lay ahead. With one long lick, he moved right past her thigh and to that place some call "home." She became immediately more receptive. Pac then flipped her over and mounted her from the rear. This time Cat began devouring J's lollipop, and the three of them continued as before.

Sex, sex, sex. The three of them did it all. Fucking, sucking, screwing, licking, bucking, rubbing, caressing, making love, making whoopee, having intercourse, reproducing, achieving coitus, biting, scratching, and slapping. It went on and on, on and on. All three began moaning loudly and yelping as the tension mounted.

But within the sounds of their sex play was a deeper, raspier moan. This deeper, rougher moan began to drown out their own sex sounds. It grew to a fever pitch until they stopped altogether and looked over to the side of the bed.

There was T-dog, with both hands wrapped around his goods, furiously masturbating. He had apparently been watching the threesome and had gotten worked up. Now, his eyes were closed, and he was in his own world. He began yelping and bucking, and before the frozen porno stars could make a move, he released his white love juice all over the three of them.

"What the fuck!" Pac screamed as the goo landed all over his back.

"Oh, gross," Cat shouted out, drops of stuff dripping from her hair.

"You fucker. Now I've totally sobered up," J said as he looked at the white sticky stuff that had landed on his chest hair.

The three of them moved apart and solemnly cleaned up. T-dog just sat there, looking at them, seemingly impressed that he had managed to shoot his wad on all three of them.

Having cleaned themselves up, the four of them gathered around the table and began snacking on some string cheese.

J began, *"That was some crazy shit. I didn't know crack could make me so horny."*

98

"Hey, T-dog," Cat queried, *"did you like our little show?"*

"Yeah, actually, I did. But how'd you like my show?"

"I can't believe you shot your load on us," Pac interrupted. *"Why'd you do that shit?"*

"Well, you know," T-dog answered coyly, *"everyone has their roles to play."*

And thus, there they were. Four crack smokers. Four porno stars. Just four average college graduates in America. Redefining stereotypes and transcending boundaries. Undoubtedly, the four would go on to live out their own lives. The family, the house, the cars, the career. The stereotypical life of the middle class would find them, as it finds almost everyone eventually. But one thing is certain. For a brief moment in time, they left the cares and concerns of society behind. The "went for theirs" and did what they wanted to do.

Not everyone has the opportunity to perceive life from a new angle. Perhaps only a select few have the chance to open their doors of perception. The rest just move along blindly like rats in a maze. Indeed, this is the way it has to be. In fiction, as well as in life, everyone has their roles to play.

Fall 1997

STUCK
||||||||

"So, here we are," said the doctor. "Now what?"

"You're the psychiatrist," the lady said. "You tell us."

"Well, all right. This is kind of new for me. I'm used to hearing about the problems of others, not talking about my problems."

"Look, we're all stuck here, so we might as well hear about your fuckin' problems, you sonnafa bitch!" said the man.

"Take it easy. Take it easy, guy. No need to get so harsh," the doctor said.

"Just tell us your problems," continued the woman. "We don't have all day. Well, actually, we do."

All three of them snickered.

The doctor took a deep breath and began. "OK, let's see...Let me start from the beginning. As you both know, my name is Dr. Nachumi, and I am a full-time psychiatrist at the Manhattan Psychiatric Center. My field of specialty is substance abuse, but as you both know, over the last few years, I've been counseling couples with sexual problems."

"Hey, motherfucker," the man interrupted, "you said you were gonna start from the beginning. This sounds more like the end."

"Or at least the middle," the woman added.

"OK, OK. You two sure are harsh. Let me start again." The doctor clasped his two meaty hands together as if he were pondering. His fat, chunky nose tilted side to side like a confused toucan. "Four score and seven years ago, our founding fathers put forth this—"

"What the hell are you talking about?" the woman interrupted. "I'm sick of this. I want to get the hell out of here."

"Well, you can't. So just shut the hell up. We're gonna be stuck here for a long fucking time." The man was Weaze Fontaine, a dark, skinny Indian guy from Florida with a knack for the foulest of language. He had these bulging eyes and a peculiar expression on his face most of the time. And when he laughed, it was obvious. He was crazy.

"Fanny, why don't you tell the doctor a little bit more about yourself," Weaze suggested. "After all, you're the fucking reason we're here, anyway."

"Fuck you, Weaze," she retorted. "We're not here just for me. I might have my problems, but at least I'm not a schizophrenic."

The woman was Fanny Fontaine, a blonde-haired, blue-eyed, Southern-accented Virginian. She was blessed with a beautiful, well-sculpted body and cursed with poor judgment. Perhaps the biggest mistake in her young, passionate life was to marry Weaze. Besides being a foul-mouthed, double-talking, shady used-car salesman, Weaze was also a diagnosed schizophrenic.

All of a sudden, there was a loud knock at the door.

"Well, I guess this is it," Dr. Nachumi said. "All good things must come to an end."

Then the door was thrown open, and three firemen came in.

"What the hell?" Fireman #1 said.

His walkie-talkie chirped. "This is the captain. What's going on in there?"

"Well, Captain," he said, "it seems we have three naked people here. There's a blonde girl on her side, with an Indian guy facing her, with his thing in her vagina, and a fat white guy behind her, with his thing in her ass. They appear to be stuck."

"Uh, please repeat...I'm not sure if I heard you right. Please repeat," chirped the captain through the walkie-talkie.

Fireman #1 repeated the description.

At first, there was silence, and then some more chirping from the walkie-talkie. "Get the lube-of-life. That's their only chance."

"Yes, Captain, right away."

"This is so embarrassing," Fanny said.

While Fireman #1 went to get the necessary tools to pry them apart, Fireman #2 kneeled down next to the trio.

"So, how did this happen?"

"Oh, I can tell you how this fucking happened!" Weaze offered. "You see, Fanny and I came to this quack for some counseling. Our love life hasn't been too great lately. This fucker starts talking to us. Then he gives us some pills; then, a half hour later, we're all horny and emotional. So Fanny and I start doing it right there on the floor. Then before we know it, Dr. Porno over here slides up behind and sticks it in her ass."

"And because of the venous engorgement in the erectile tissue," adds Dr. Nachumi, "we were not able to separate."

1998

HOUSE OF LUNACY, PART I

||||||||||||||||||||||||||||||||||||||||

See us rising
Like a rocket or a comet
Screaming through the night
Are you fantasizing
About the lights in your eyes
As you ride us
Deep inside
A darkened building
You climb some stairs
And climb some more
You're gasping for breath
And you just got to the front door
Knock knock
BOOM BOOM
Bass in your face
Red and blue lights all over
Bodies all over the place
And soon for you the taste
You like it green
You like it sweet
You like white sauce
With your dark meat
Throw off your clothes with us
Nobody knows like us
Inhibitions are the only fee
Welcome to the House of Lunacy

Jerry Curls
December 1997

HOUSE OF LUNACY, PART II
||||||||||||||||||||||||||||||||||

I wait for the night to come
So I can spray up my dust
Because it's just feasibly easy
Oh, let the sun go down
Round these streets we run
One-on-one or two-on-one
Up under these sheets it's fun
Bring back the tricks and treats
From the street
House of Lunacy bound are we
Found, put the green and the white stuff down
Now we need it
On your knees
Push it in and believe it
See, this is the tale of the Lewnatics
And the jamz, jamz-jammy-jamz
Uproarious, glorious
Spirits beyond eternity
Death won't come easy
So don't look for us, cuz
We're slippery, magically, mystically
Tucked away like a mouse in a faraway galaxy
Known to some as the House of Lunacy.

April 9, 1998

104

THE DEN
||||||||||

Settle down, boys and girls, and let me tell you a story. The year is 1997, and the place is Brooklyn, New York. Let us focus in on a shady and perhaps sleazy apartment in an area known as Bay Ridge. It is here where the denizens of the underworld congregate and partake of many unholy activities. Ah, yes, boys and girls, I fuckin' remember it well.

Even the buzzer on the door was different. For all the other apartments, there was a standard black button buzzer. But for this apartment, there was a big white box with a button, which triggered a doorbell chime. Now, if you were lucky enough to be buzzed into The Den, the first "person" you would meet was the dog. I can't remember his name right now, or maybe I'm trying to block it out. You see, the dog and I never got along. He was too hyper. Every time someone was fucking, the dog would get all excited and start barking and running around. That was enough to kill a hard-on. But enough about the dog.

The first thing that hit you (after the dog) was the smoke—the smoke of cigarettes, the smoke of weed, the smoke of food. The smoke of food would come from the kitchen, which was on the right as you entered and walked down the hall. Now, I hate describing decorations and the layout of a room. But I have to describe this room, because this place was fucked up. The living room table was a circular slab of wood that you could spin. This was a handy option. Instead of having to pass an item (such as the salt, a fork, a beer, or the bong), you could spin the table, and the person in need could just pick it up. Of course, you might also put down a full bottle of beer, only to pick up someone else's empty bottle five minutes later.

Now, let me break from the classic writing style. The remainder of this story will be images of The Den: naked bodies running around, penises going into vaginas...in, out, in, out, a little of the old in-out, in-out...crack smoke puffed into the dog's face, lines of blow, sniff, sniff, sniff, sniff...naked body in the shower getting a blow job...stereo surround sound...so much food, so much fucking food.

Why can't places like this last forever?

June 2, 2001

FOUR-EYED SAND NIGGA
||||||||||||||||||||||||||||||||||

Real OGs
Don't stop 'cause we can't stop.
Smoother than a breeze in the West Indies,
Listen to me while I spit on thee.

Back in elementary,
Mean kids made fun of me.
But now, look who got fucked?
You're puttin' in work at Mickey D's,
While I'm makin' green
From LA to the NYC.

This little four-eyed sand nigga
Is on a roll, nigga.
Now my mama drives a Rolls, nigga.
So now what d'you wanna do, fool?

You're fuckin' with me?
See what real terrorists can do.
Hear the sounds of my bomb go *blauw!*
Hezbollah runs this shit now.

October 19, 1997

I AM, THEREFORE I THINK
||||||||||||||||||||||||||||||||||||||

"All of a sudden, I'm alive!" she said.

"That's because the moment you spoke, you were, in a sense, created," replied the old man.

"I don't understand. What do you mean?"

"Well, five seconds before you said you were alive, you did not exist. Now, the writer has given you life. You are having a conversation with me, an old man. As long as this piece of paper is not destroyed, this conversation will become part of the 'written word.' Thus, you and I have become immortal."

"Wow! That's amazing. And all because of this writer guy."

"Yes, the writer has created you, and he decides what will happen to you. This small conversation could be part of a large novel. You could actually become a very well-known character in a weekly newspaper series. I might become the wise old man whom heroes refer to in an epic series of books by the very same writer. It's all possible. Anything can happen."

"This is all so very exciting. Five minutes ago, I was nothing, and now, I exist. You're telling me that I could be anything the writer wants me to be. I could be a beautiful ballerina, or the princess of a great castle, or the Queen of England, or even a hot-blooded college girl in a steamy romance novel.

You mean to tell me I could be any one of these people, and this conversation could be just a small part in my lengthy chronicle of existence?"

"Yes, this is all possible. But look, lady, since the writer is writing this on a subway and his stop is coming up, your fantasies will have to wait. For now, you're nothing but another stupid bitch."

March 28, 1997

PAROLE
|||||||||

Six months till the end of this jail sentence.

As I sit in this hotel on Central Park West, looking at all these stuffed mummies, I begin to drift. But before I drift off, a waiter is questioned by one of the ladies at my table.

"What kind of wine is this?"

"Well, ma'am, it's from California."

"Ah, California," she retorts.

Ah, California, I scream in my own head. California—dreams of California. Dreams of sunshine, beaches, scantily clad women in bikinis. Dreams of convertibles...

My thoughts are interrupted again by a conversation at the next table.

A dorky-looking guy is talking about his wife.

"So, I'm gonna take my wife to California."

The Beginning

2001

WHERE'S LITTLE ITALY?

||||||||||||||||||||||||||||||||||

Forza Italia
Leisurely stroll we
The corner of Grand and Mulberry
Spaghetti-hair Guido
Call me Vinnie, Sal, or Babarino
Feed me, stuff me, please me
Calzone and pizza says my belly
Tiramisu and angel-hair linguine

Egg rolls? Chow mein? Fish market?
Lost are we
But the map says it's so
Above Canal Street
And not below
Deep in the heart of the Bowery
These Italians look Chinese
Chinatown has eaten Little Italy.

December 21, 1997

RESURRECTION

||||||||||||||||||

This is dedicated to Ben Zandpour (1973–1997).
Rest in pieces
Resurrection (re-zer-rek'shon) n. - a rising again; the rising of the dead at judgment time.

Tuesday night, December 23, 1997

Murder was the case
Suicide was the fate
All men must fall
This blood's on all y'all
Blame it on my friends
They killed me
Izzy Bar
See how far
One can fall
Can't stand tall
With my dad's sweater on my chest
Like a bulletproof vest
Laugh it up
Laugh it up
Shun me
As I pucker up
First the man takes a drink
Then the drink takes a drink
Then the drink takes the man
Master plan
Shut up and listen
My blood poetry bleeds
This untold story

Gang up, gang up, gang up
Gang up and kill me
If you want to laugh
Don't look to me
No clowns here
Only my blood poetry
An "uptight Kike," she called me
Get it right
I'm Islamic Middle Eastern
And if one word sums me up
It's "sexy"
Look around
My homies playin' me out
Gamin' me out
Sellin' me out
What can I say
Hey, hey
Et tu, Brute
Now shut up and listen
First the man takes a drink
Then the drink takes a drink
Then the drink takes a man
Understand
You got the digits from the "bitches"
But look, I'm making riches
Jack Daniels in my veins
Mixed with Indo and Yayo
I'm insane
Blughh...blugh, blughhh
Throwing up chunks from my belly
And this nosebleed
Ah, Lord, help me
Praying to the Porcelain God

Driving the Porcelain Bus
Leave us neighbor
Can't you hear I'm dry heaving
On the bathroom floor
Dying, dying
Death at age 24
Who for and what for
Live by the street life
Die by the street life
Close my eyes
Watch my life pass by
High school
Never forget the "sorrow"
College
"Awakening"
Feel my body breathing
Med school
"The War"
Struggle
Like never seen before
My life, my life, my life
Passes by
Inhale, Exhale
Inhale——Exhale
In—
Nope
My last breath
Now comes the death
Death
Death
Death
Death

Death
Death
Death
Death
"KROY WEN" killed me.

"Oh, Mother, I can feel the soil falling over my head."

Darkness.
Then, a light
Dim, but growing bright
Sounds.
Faint, but growing strong.
"Push, push, push on."
"Here it comes; here it comes."
Through the tunnel
Whooosh! And then
Splaaaaash!
"Congratulations...It's a boy."

Everything is so clear now.
Liquidity and lucidity.
I'm a made man now.
Untouchable.
Nothing will ever be the same.
Resurrection.

Do you know what it's like to die?

New Year's Day 1998

DOCTORS AND RAPPERS
||||||||||||||||||||||||||||||||||

Four o' clock in the morning,
Grab my white coat and my stethoscope,
I take the 5 Train to Brooklyn.
Six days a week, it's how I'm living.

I'm in a Fantasy Land.
I'm in a Prison Land.
Some people die in my arms,
And some people die alone.

B.I.G. P.O.P.P.A.
Is a dead muthafucka now, yay-yayee.
Now look how 2Pac died.
Two hip-hop stars laid down on the Westside.
I'm tickety tongue-tied with my head down, way down.
Lord, what'ch you gotta fuck with us for?

1997

DEATH CLOUD
||||||||||||||||||

There is a death cloud around everyone. I'm not trying to be morbid, but it's true. Imagine an invisible cloud of death hovering over you, enveloping you, 360 degrees. The thickness and closeness of the cloud to you is all dependent on how close you are to death.

For example, when you're driving on the freeway, the death cloud permeates. Thick and close to you, the death cloud surrounds you. One wrong move, and an eighteen-wheeler will flatten your spine.

Three years ago, in New York, we witnessed one of the largest death clouds ever televised.

Close your eyes. Can you see it? Can you see your death cloud hovering, lingering, waiting for you?

September 11, 2004

LIFE AT 2159 EAST 2ND ST.
IIIIIIIIIIIIIIIIIIIIIIIIIIIIIIIIIIIIIII

Demesmerize me, demesmerize me.
Demesmerize me, demesmerize me.

As I walk around this town,
I think to myself
Brooklyn South is hell-bound.
Old men and old women
Just trying to get around.

Wheelchairs, canes, walkers.
Take a step. Step, step.
Take a step. Step, step.
One step closer to death.

Just rolling down the avenue, Avenue U.
Looking for something or someone to get into.
Is that a beautiful face around the bend?
Fuck no. This is Grave's End.

Someone once told me that
Coney Island is mesmerizing.
Well, if this is mesmerizing,
Then won't you please demesmerize me?

May 14, 1997

BEST SIDE STORY
||||||||||||||||||||||||

A red-and-gold sky
The plane touches down
LAX.
California.

It's seventy degrees
And it's January
Just another day in California.
Drop the top down.
And feel the heat
This is Inglewood,
California.

The Big Apple
Has a worm in it
So I'm leaving it
For California.
The BQE
And the Belt Parkway
Hunks of junk
Not in California.

The 405
And Interstate 5
We call them "freeways"
In California.

Rodeo Drive
Not 5th Avenue
Beverly Hills,
California.

Step off Broadway
This is Sunset Boulevard
Hollywood,
California.

Back to the beach
Suntan lotion
Dental floss bikinis
California.
Newport Beach
Huntington Beach
Laguna Beach,
California.

Venice beach
Long beach
Malibu,
California.

Pineapples and avocados
Palm trees and burritos
The Golden State
California.

Surf City
Here I come
Coppertone me up.
California

The Lakers, the Bruins,
The Trojans and the Raiders
Play ball
In California.

My heart in San Francisco
Fisherman's Wharf
Fuck South Street Seaport
This is California.

Persian power
Runs Irvine like the mafia
Little Tehran City,
California
Humboldt State
This bud's for you
The strongest herb on the planet
Stoned in California

Hummers and Ferraris
Low riders and Lamborghinis
Cars for the stars
California
Much love and respect
For the place that made me
The land that raised me
California.

Peace to the East
But take back my key
Let me live my life
Where summer is the only season

LA is the only reason
Mama, I'm coming home
Westside till I die!

California

January 15, 1998

GRENADA

||||||||||||||||||||||||||||||||

GRENADA: AN INTRODUCTION
|||||||||||||||||||||||||||||||||||||||||

Welcome, brave reader! You are about to enter a world beyond the scope of human imagination. A world of such unknown depth and dimensions that your very mortal fiber will find itself removed from your soul like so much string cheese taken from a baby's crib on an average afternoon day in a Polish deli in Manhattan. See what I mean? You are truly about to embark on a most serious quest. Along the way, you will encounter passion, fury, excitement, pain, frustration, and eventually, sauerkraut.

Well, if you've come with me to this point, you must have some interest in this voyage. So, as your humble narrator, let me explain what exactly is happening. There once was a young chap named Ben Zandpour. He made a trip—no, he went on the adventure of a thousand lifetimes. He plummeted into the hottest fires of hell. He flew above the most joyous domains of heaven. What you are reading now is only a mere introduction to the saga of one human being. During the course of your reading, you might find yourself riveted. You might find yourself watery-eyed. You might find yourself questioning your own existence. However, above all else, never underestimate the value of sauerkraut. It really is a wonder food, which goes well with virtually all dishes, from hot dogs to chocolate cheesecake.

The basic format of this tour de force, this legendary tale of woe, this firmament, this England, is in the form of a collection of short stories, poems, abstracts, and other literary canvases. Feel free to read them in any order you prefer. Each piece should be relatively independent of other pieces. You may find that some of the material appeals to your bowels, others to your genitals, some to your mind, others to your sense of dread, some to your heart, and others to your sense of fashion. Anyway, I've rambled on for long enough. Buckle your seat belts and prepare for the ultimate pilgrimage. Foolish mortals...

June 4, 1995

THE INCIDENT
||||||||||||||||

REPORTER : What do you call yourself?
CITIZEN : JAMZ.

REPORTER : How do you feel about what has happened here today?
CITIZEN : How do I feel about it? How the fuck am I supposed to feel about it? You want me to tell you that I'm sorry, that I regret what happened. Actually, I'm kind of glad it happened.

REPORTER : Given your high degree of education, don't you feel that your actions were a bit unwarranted?

CITIZEN : I thought we agreed that you wouldn't ask any loaded questions.

REPORTER : Perhaps I should rephrase the question. Could you tell me a little bit about the factors that led up to this incident?

CITIZEN : It's like this: I came to this country in search of a medical education, a medical education that the United States could not provide. That's it. That's the only reason I came. I had no idea that I would have to deal with a weasel-like food salesman posing as a student who would constantly hound me day and night, trying to sell me all kinds of marked-up bullshit just to make a few extra pennies. And so, I'm glad I chopped his head off with my machete while he slept.

REPORTER : JAMZ, are you ready to spend the rest of your life in prison?

CITIZEN : There is nothing prison can do to me that the Rock hasn't done already.

June 4, 1995

CRABBACK: A GRENADIAN DELICACY

||||||||||||||||||||||||||||||||||||||||||||||||

In the beginning, there was only black. And it was good. The Earth spinned slowly in its peaceful darkness, while the animals within it grew and prospered. The mud and the dirt of the gentle Earth offered protection and support for the land-dwelling creatures of the night. These creatures toiled and were industrious under this soft land, digging elaborate passageways and numerous underground dwellings. Different animals dominated the land on different parts of the planet. One island in particular was dominated by a certain hardy species of life. These organisms bore tough, thick, calcified exoskeletons and sharp, slicing claws. In their arsenal, they stored the different textures and compositions of this small island's soil and created hidden passageways under the ground, with only the occasional opening into the upper world. These sturdy, hard-working entities grew and prospered, and came to be known as the land crabs.

June 1995

THE PRESSURE COOKER
|||||||||||||||||||||||||||||||

Bulging and pushing at the sides
Glistening with steam
Another piece of beef stew
Into the pressure cooker.

Throw in some vegetables.
Throw in some carrots.
Fucking throw it all in
And watch it boil.

Stir it all up
A dash of Tobasco
Make it real hot
But DON'T LET ANY STEAM OUT!

Let's take a taste
And share the porridge
A dinner for kings and queens

No, No, No, No, No!
Talk about it,
But don't eat it!

St. George's University

October 9, 1995

SHITTING IN THE WOODS
||||||||||||||||||||||||||||||||||

Some green leaves fell off the tree today. The rain sprinkled down from the heavens, making today a rather gloomy Saturday. I'm sick of starting stories with some bull-shit description of the weather. Let me get to the point.

I decided to go running because I was restless. Actually, I was bored out of my fucking mind. So I put on my Adidas (insert ad here), and I was on my way. I was feeling a little bit on the wild side on this particular evening. Maybe it was because of the full moon. I'm talking about a really fat, bloated full moon, a full moon only worthy of the country-Caribbean darkness of Grenada.

So, anyway, I go running down True Blue Road, skip-ping over random potholes and puddles, which always make my runs a bit treacherous, only to come to a fork in the road. I have encountered this same fork every time I go running. But this time, since I was feeling a little bit on the wild side— "the road less traveled," blah, blah, blah—I decided to go on the right.

I was having a good run. But I felt heavy. I'd eaten a big lunch earlier that day. Mexican food. Being in a third-world country in the middle of the night, one gets creative.

So I squatted near a bush and had a bowel movement. A burrito. A big burrito. And the best part...It was clean, as I found out later.

Wasn't that a good story?

October 1995/October 2004

THE FIRST DAY
||||||||||||||||||||

Jerry C. woke with a start. He had been dreaming of bod-ies in the moonlight, writhing in the sand, and momentarily, he couldn't remember where he was. Then the soft voice of the flight attendant called to him through his somnolent haze, gently reminding him to bring his seat back to the full, upright position and stow the rest, lest they need to repri-mand him during final approach. Outside the double-paned windows, a sky like acid-washed denim hung over the water, which rippled and gleamed through shades of aqua green and kiss me I'm blue—winking sunlight back to his tired, red-rimmed eyes. Pressing his cheek to the glasstic as the plane banked in a slow, lazy circle, Jerry spied the island.

It sprang from the sea in a great tumult of rock and green-ery, rising like a half-melted cone of pineapple-lime sher-bet, daubed with marzipan beaches and rock-candy bluffs. A brief glimpse of red-roofed St. George's, weaving its ten-drils up from the marina into the hills, and then the plane was circling around the north end of the island, lush and wild, exuberant Atlantic breakers crashing against the bluffs of Carib's Leap, where, hundreds of years before, an entire tribe of natives chose freedom in a watery grave over sub-servience under an imperialist fist.

Like an improbable jet engine on a stone on the end of an invisible line of rope, the jet swung around the island, curv-ing in a wide arc to the southwest. Jerry thought he could make out the school—several tiled-roofed buildings perched atop a high hill, surrounded by clearings and construction. A few buildings stood perilously close to the water's edge, high above a tiny black-sand beach. A finger of land jutted south, tapering to a point, and beyond that, Jerry could just make out a small, flat island, but then all he saw was sea.

The captain warned the flight attendants to take their seats. Jerry squashed his nose up against the window, trying to see the runway he assumed was somewhere up ahead. Nothing but more water. It was admittedly a gorgeous color, but there was too much of it, and it rose up to meet them awfully quickly. Just when he was about to put his head down in the KYA-good-bye position, a quick flash of white, then gray, and the solidly satisfying jarring thunk as the big jet touched down on the Cuban-built, marine-liberated tarmac of the Point Salines Airport's main and only runway. The rising howl of the turbofans as they slowed the airliner masked Jerry's sigh as he closed his eyes and sank back into his seat. *Well*, he thought, *I'm here. And I got here on a jumbo.*

When the bell chimed and the light winked out, the entire planeload of people leaped from their seats in a mad scramble for carry-ons packed away in overstuffed over-head compartments. They elbowed and clawed at each other, cramming themselves into the aisles, the pressure building like a pistoning rod waiting for the door to open, spewing them onto the tarmac in an orgasmic release. Jerry C. watched from his seat, bemused.

"They're all gunners, man." Jerry turned to the sound of the voice. His seatmate pointed at the struggling mass. "Those are the ones who'll do anything and everything to make the grade. They're all honey in your face, but when you turn your back..." His fingers became a nine. *Pow!*

"How do I know you're not a gunner?" Jerry asked.

"I'm Dar, man," he said as a small woman fell backward onto his lap. She smiled at him, impishly blowing her wavy blonde hair out of her green eyes. "I'm Dar, miss," he said to her as he helped her to her feet with a casual hand on her rear.

"I'm Farrah," she said with just enough of a trace of Brooklyn to be sexy. Just then, the door popped open, and with a sigh, the passengers filed out. "See you later." Farrah smiled again as she was swept away on the tide of duffel bags and knapsacks.

"I'm going to like it here," said Dar. He tied a blue bandanna over his bald brown head and slid on opaque wraparound shades. As the last carry-on rolled by, Dar stood and pulled a large guitar from the overhead compartment. "Let's get warm."

"How did you...?" Jerry started to ask, mentally trying to do the math as he struggled to extricate his rolling carry-on from the tiny overhead bin. He stopped himself and smiled, knowing the answer. He was Dar, man.

He followed Dar out of the plane, pausing momentarily to kiss his favorite flight attendant good-bye. He stepped out onto the stairway.

Heat and humidity struck him hard, forcing the last of the air-conditioned air out of him with a whoosh. He squinted into the light, wishing he hadn't packed his shades in his suitcase.

The pilot had parked the jet in a seemingly random spot of the tarmac. A line of passengers meandered into the terminal, struggling with leviathan carry-ons. A group of dark men in pale-blue shorts wrestled with beached whale–sized luggage from the cargo hold.

The single terminal building was low and wide. Small children waved and shouted from a terrace overlooking the entrance to customs. To one side, the runway abruptly ended at a chain-link fence. On the other side of the fence ran a small dirt road where a group of people sat in jeeps, watching impassively, drinking. In the other direction, the long, wide runway stretched out. Designed to handle the bulk of anything from Cessnas to C5 Galaxies (or their Soviet equivalents), its smooth, pale surface rolled straight and true out the end of the land itself, beyond which only the sea sparkled in the dazzling sun. A single red light flashed its warning of an impending cliff.

Jerry followed Dar down the hot metal stairway and across the tarmac, heat rising through the rubber soles of his Converse All Stars. As they approached the terminal, Jerry scanned the faces of the crowd lining the rails above. Smiling faces laughed and cheered, family and friends, grim-looking men in uniform searched for matching profiles. Jerry's eyes fell upon someone watching him—a wizened, leathery man, skin of shining ebony, hair gray and black, falling in thick dreadlocks along his back. His eyes were dark-black pools, ribboned with red. He smiled at Jerry, gold tooth gleaming in the sun. A shiver passed through Jerry, like a cold, wet hug that engulfed him, seeping into him until it chilled his very bones. Jerry shuddered and blinked, but when he looked back, the man was gone.

"State your business, please."

"I'm a student at the medical school."

"First time here?"

"Um, yes."

"Letter of intent."

"Um, here."

"This is a letter from your mother."

"Sorry, here."

"Did you bring more than ten thousand US dollars cash?"

"No."

"Did you bring electronic items or food that you would or could sell or trade?"

"Yes...I mean, no...I mean, yes, I brought electronics and food, but I'm not going to sell them."

"So you're going to trade them?"

"No."

"But you could."

"What? Well, I suppose I could."

"Do you possess any medication, prescription or nonprescription pills, tablets, suppositories, creams, tinctures, cocaine, emollients, capsules, weed, speed, crack, or Pepto-Bismol?"

"I'm not sure how to answer that, so I'll say no."

"You realize that if you lie to me or are found with any contraband or possibly fit the profiles here listed on the form you signed, you may be subject to detention and deportation?"

"So I've heard."

"How long are you going to be staying?"

"Well, two years, but not all at once."

"You realize that you cannot stay longer than thirty days."

"But I'm supposed to be here for at least six months. It says so in the letter."

"We will see. Now, proceed to baggage claim. Enjoy your stay and get good grades. Do not lose your visa!"

Jerry C. took back his freshly stamped passport and visa, and wandered into baggage claim. Behind him, he heard Dar being waved through with a hearty "Good luck, mon." Jerry shook his head and greeted Dar.

They stood watching the parade on the baggage carousel. They had both read the pamphlets the school sent out, full of gloss and glory, promising a thoroughly relaxing education in a tropical paradise. They had also read the messages from previous students, detailing the dire and dramatic differences life on a small tropical island would hold in store for the coddled, overfed, and clueless students from America. This would be no vacation fun in the sun. They would have to study hard, bring down their own books, supplies, snacks, soap, and other sundries of civilization. And when the electricity (220 volt, of course) went out, they would swelter without fans or air-conditioning; they would study by lamp and candlelight under heavy netting caked with deet to repel the diseased *Aedes aegypti*, the mosquito that carries dengue fever. It was said the first time you got it, you would suffer extreme, wrenching pain, the breakbone fever that mercifully subsided after a couple of weeks. But if you were unfortunate enough to be vampirized again, things could get hemorrhagic. Your body would start to bruise, and you would bleed from your nose, eyes, and rectum. Your skin would jaundice and swell as your liver and spleen shut down, and you would die a slow, painful death as every red blood cell in your body spontaneously ruptured and left your blood stream to color your deathbed shroud red and brown and black. Deep Woods Off! was a hot commodity that first month.

Jerry C. watched patiently as his fellow students and their worried parents, SOs' spouses, and family, plucked their cases packed with paper, pens, Pop-Tarts, lamps, hair dryers, generators, sewing machines, stereos, CDs, TVs and VCRs, shorts, shirts, stockings, beef jerky, and cans of everything from asparagus to Spam to yams. Someone pulled what appeared to be a collapsible Quonset hut off the belt. A small, soft, red suitcase went round and round. Dar grabbed two large duffel bags, each emblazoned with a skull and crossbones on a field shaped like a Japanese maple. He flashed Jerry the peace sign and then headed for the growing customs line.

After some time, new bags stopped emerging from the magic portal, and the number of bags dwindled. The little red suitcase went round and round. Then the conveyor stopped, and the overhead speaker crackled something unintelligible. Jerry and several other distraught passengers accosted a tired-looking airline representative. "We are sorry," he said, "but due to the enormous volume of baggage checked in, some of your bags were left in Puerto Rico or perhaps diverted back to Miami or Jamaica. Please check back tomorrow or the next day with your claim checks to see if they've come in on a later flight."

"How could this have happened? Couldn't you have used a bigger plane?"

"We did use a bigger plane in anticipation of this increased load, but this year's group just packed too much stuff. Come back tomorrow. Thank you for flying American." With that, the representative disappeared into a secret doorway and was later spotted with colleagues at the local bar on the beach, red-eyed and laughing, Carib beer in hand.

So Jerry C. went to customs, and though he had nothing to declare, a somber but courteous customs officer efficiently searched every orifice before ejecting him through the frosted-glass doors into the heat of the streets of Grenada.

He was immediately surrounded by a clamoring throng of tourists, students, porters, guides, vendors, taxi drivers, and some shifty-eyed individuals whose function wasn't immediately apparent. Jerry scanned the crowd, wondering what to do next. Suddenly, a tanned young man in Bermuda shorts, a T-shirt, and small round shades grabbed him by the shoulder. "True Blue of Grand Anse?" he asked cryptically.

Jerry could only muster a "Huh?" in response.

"Are you at the True Blue or Grand Anse campus?" the man asked again. "You're a student, right?"

Jerry nodded.

"Welcome to Grenada," said the man. "I'm Mike. I'm a fourth termer." Mike checked Jerry's name against a list and chuckled. "Sorry, man, you're in the barracks. Wait over there." He gestured to his right and moved on, with an over-the-shoulder "Good luck."

Jerry moved over to a milling group of new students, most of whom appeared to be in their mid-twenties, mostly white or brown, and mostly male. They stood alone in pairs, some with parents, a few with children. Dressed like tourists—in shorts, polo shirts, Birkenstocks, and hats, and sweating profusely—they chatted nervously. Jerry, not feeling particularly conversational, listened, picking up random snippets.

"Yeah, I applied pretty late, and by the time I was ready, most of the schools were done."

"I had good grades, but my MCATS weren't so hot."

"I interviewed with Dr. J himself, and he fast-tracked me."

"I'm scared."

To be continued...

LEW
Circa 1997

Monk Hood
||||||||||||||||

Gregor and Thelonius
Sat vexed (or was it waxed?)
Within the snug, cozy concrete
Of their hilltop abode.

> A soft serpent stole someone's soul somewhere.
> Sometime.

"Guerillas can't get me."
As the monk's Uzis
Purrrrrred the hillside.
The phat TARGETS were promptly 187'ed.

Axed, loc'd, and vexed
(And maybe even waxed)
The pipe-hittin' Peniles
Faxed a fish to a PuSSYcAt

Left hand black
The long, sharp pinky nail
Pierced a snack
From around her back.
        (Who's the mack?)

> A soft serpent stole someone's soul somewhere.
> Sometime.

A sharp, but so very dull,
Bluish pain screamed,
     "Please let me free, ma'am!"
Whirling, spinning, kicking.
       Biting.

Fuck Grenada

January 10, 1995

MISS LEWIS
||||||||||||||

I would write a poem
But I'm all "tied up"
To an island green
With fruity trees that I speak of.

Dance, dance at Fantasia
And I betcha it'll letcha
Grin and jump, jump and prance.
Is there romance in Grenada?

El tocador de Venezuela
Toca la guitarra. Que bonita!
And there was "Murder in the Streets,"
Which offered food for the mind, but nothing to eat.

Coney Island, the big fair
Hair, where? Good things must end.
Yes, I'm there.
And in the end, I've made a friend.

June 8, 1995

A BIT OF NARRATION
|||||||||||||||||||||||||||||

Four a.m. She kicked me out again. And this time I really don't know why. Oh well, time to head back to True Blue. Hitching a ride at this hour in Grenada is just about as easy as getting into a US medical school. As I walked along Lagoon Road on an average hot and humid Caribbean night, with the Caribbean Sea on my right and some jungle on my left, I noticed a figure approaching.

"Johnson, what's up?"
"Yes, Doc. Comin' from your lady friend's?"
"That's right, and what are you doin'?"
"I lookin' for some eats. Might you give me five dollars?"
"I only have two, man."
"OK. Thanks, Doc. Have a sugar cane. Just suck the juice out."
"All right, man, thanks. Take it easy and stay up."
"Wise words, one love."

It's funny how I would always run into Johnson (aka Charles, a bum whom I had known for over a year) at the strangest times. I walked for quite some time, having sucked my sugar cane nearly dry, when finally someone stopped for me. As I sat snugly in the left-sided passenger seat with my sugar buzz, the driver babbled something about his travels of the world, and I thought to myself,

Just another night in Grenada City, California.

November 9, 1995

144

IMPRO
||||||||

Pizow, I move from the Westside.
Ganja Totin'
And the muthafuckin' drive-by.
Slip out back and around again.
I smoke crack.
Fuck the juice and the gin.
And I come-alistic
With the ride...slide...
Southern Playalistic
With the realistic
Motion, Grenada lotion
Persian love potion.

December 23, 1995

GRENADA BABBLE
||||||||||||||||||||||||||

Twice upon a time, in a land far, far away, there were two of everything. Two birthdays, two dozen hot chicks/guys, two giant breasts with whipped cream drooling down the sides and hot fudge burning the nipples. There, he found out *she* was a transvestite who had a fondness for coconut cream pies and Grenadian guys. *He* had a fondness for coconut cream pies with hot fudge! But no beer, wine, sangria, rum, whiskey, tequila, chablis, bloody marys, ham, bacon, or sausage because these things were harmful to one's soul.

When he whipped out the giant lizard and let it run loose, she took off her red leather G-string and put it over his turban. He unrolled his beard and used it as a sling to support all twelve inches of his throbbing love muscle. Then he removed the dick turban and told her it would be her honor to suck it. But first, she lathered it with hot sauce and tortilla chips. Suddenly, she looked up with great delight as she slung his cobra into her temple of doom. She squealed with delight.

As the walls of the temple of doom closed in...another chilling scream...the cobra squeezed to death...The dark, powerful temple claims another victim. Who shall be the next victim? Jim, Irfan, Frank, Krishna...Irfan. Yes, Irfan it shall be. The walls of the temple beckoned.

"Irfan, come to me."

All of a sudden, Buffy (Irfan) died, due to too much lifting and no exercise. T-bob rose from his slumber and became ruler of the universe, otherwise known as GADH.

146

My dog was gay, so I killed the bitch. But it didn't die. It got up and wanted some bone. Some big, fat, juicy bone. The dog was so horny it didn't know whether to eat the bone or screw itself. The dog sat there, holding the bone in its paw, realizing it had drunk too much rum punch and proceeded to vomit in the middle of the...

THE END

1995

PED'S
IIIIIIII

We filed into the small, hot room, one by one, not really knowing what was in store for us. The room had a stale-blood
stench, and there was no air-conditioning. As I positioned
myself against a wall, I noticed that some of the others were
turning a bit pale and were having obvious difficulties with
this situation. I then focused my attention on the table in
front of me, on which lay a small three-year-old boy on his
back. He had smooth black skin and braids in his hair. I knew
something was wrong when his large brown eyes were not
drawn to my Bugs Bunny tie. His eyes just stared straight
ahead without giving the faintest recognition of anything.
His chest was completely cut open, and I could clearly see
his heart and liver. Dark-red blood was everywhere, flowing
freely from his chest like a river. One of the others began
coughing and had to leave the room.

"All right," said the woman with her gloved hands inside the
child's chest. "The inferior vena cava has been transected.
Let's turn him over."

And as they turned him over, liters of blood spilled from his
chest and splashed onto the table. Red blood everywhere.
Also, from his nostrils popped out two cotton plugs, followed
by volumes of thick, yellow, slimy mucus. They drained him
and then placed him on his back again. By now, a couple of
the others had quietly and quickly fled the room.

The woman cut the boy's small heart out of his chest and
placed it on the table. "Here's the problem," she said as she
slid her finger through a hole in the heart's wall.

148

"Yep, ventricular septal defect," said a man. "The boy never had a chance."

The woman then cut out one of the boy's lungs and placed it on the table. She cut off a small section of the lung and placed it into a bowl of water. The piece sank quickly to the bottom.

"Yep," said the same man. "This lung's as solid as a liver. A lung with air would float."

"We need to check his lateral ventricles," said another man with a saw in his hand. He placed the saw firmly to the back of the child's skull and began sawing until the head cracked open. He then pulled the skull farther apart and exposed the brains. The woman began to cut deep into the brain matter.

"Nope, no emboli. Everything's fine here."

"All right, then. Let's close him up."

They then sewed a long stitch from his belly button to his neck and another one around his skull. He was then placed in a black bag and zipped up over his head.

This was my first autopsy.

February 3, 1996

Untitled (dear white fella)
||||||||||||||||||||||||||||||||||||||||||||

Got this off the Net...Read it...Don't take offense...
Mohammad

A Poem Written by an African Shakespeare

Dear white fella
Couple things you should know
When I born, I black
When I grow up, I black
When I go in sun, I black
When I cold, I black
When I scared, I black
When I sick, I black
And when I die, I still black.

You white fella
When you born, you pink
When you grow up, you white
When you go in sun, you red
When you cold, you blue
When you scared, you yellow
When you sick, you green
And when you die, you gray.
And you have the cheek to call me colored?

Untitled (Caribbean Blue Beckoned...)

||||||||||||||||||||||||||||||||||||||||||||||||||||||||

Caribbean blue beckoned, wet and warm, as we shed our weary carapaces of doubt and knowledge and slipped into the luminescence of the day. No more genetics in an overheated, mosquito-ridden lecture hall, surrounded by four hundred of the tightest-assed niggaz med school had to offer. For the moment, we were free of all cares and worries, and we skipped, slid, and slithered to the Office—the bathroom of the True Blue Degenerates, the most misunderstood and overspeculated group of bandits in the pus-ridden class. Dorm room's vaulted ceiling strewn with TP and black light graffiti, Cypress Hill skull on the wall. Zang Bezan leaped onto the bed, combat boots shredding the mattress, lighting TP torches. His roommate Jerry lay prostrate on the floor, a forearm-sized spliff torching its own fire.

Fanny came into the room—lean, hard, and wild, with blonde hair like Axl. She pulled the jay from Jerry's lips, planted her, and sucked the smoke from his lungs. She smiled. They passed the piece, and the room shimmered and shook, and Zang looked to the wall. A beast started to call; he began to fall—right onto Fanny, who was bent over picking up a Carib bottle from the ground. He grabbed at whatever he could and felt something soft and resilient. Her ass. She closed her eyes and pushed back into his palm, and then she popped up and turned around. She looked at him and growled. Jerry said, "It is time."

They picked up their bags, sags, fags, and zigzags, and headed down the hill. All around them, students roamed hither and thither, mindlessly discussing the test and discovering they all were wrong and shitting in their Spiderman-brand Depends adult underwear. Bitches.

Fanny walked ahead of them, denim shorts tight on her ass, sculpted shoulders gleaming in the June sun. She reached back and slowly rubbed her hand up and down on Jerry's crotch. He sprang to attention. A passing student glanced down and turned away quickly, nipples hardening. They boarded the crowded student bus and bounced their way down the lush green of True Blue, headed toward Grand Anse and then...

Quick stop at the bank, the liquor store, and the drugstore to grab a sleek black reggae minivan, subwoofer pumping Buju. The plush interior was crowded, and only the backseat was free. They piled in. Tight and hot, dark and sweaty, the bus careened and bounced, and something started to get wet. Rain, rain, rain from the sky, thunderstorm bursting flash, quick as life is to die. St. George's like a Christmas tree; tonight this city belongs to me. The Carenage is full of life; good thing that Zang brought his knife. Raaaayygaaeee.

Cruising through the city, cutting through the stares. Two plus one equals three, and that's a full-ass pair. They wound their way through the market streets, crowds of faces going to places, buying fish, giving lip, what a place to start this trip. Boarded a bright-red bus driver didn't give no fuss. Shooting out north and east, leaving the little town behind, see it fading bright white and red nestled on the shore rising like a Mediterranean Lego spread straight between the legs of some pimply faced god. And around the bend, surrounded by green. The air grows cool as we rise the mountain; a parrot cuts through the sky. As they watch and lick their lips, a hawk or falcon of kite swoops in. Pretty bird good-bye. And then they leap from the still-moving bus, Fanny goosing the conductor on the way out.

On the top of the hill they stand, overlooking the foggy lake. A dormant crater. "We stand here before the Grand Etang," intoned Zang, "filled with life, teeming pond of scum fish and filth, from whence we all came." Glancing quickly around, they unzipped and let loose three yellow streams into the murky depths. Zang and Jerry watched out of the corners of their eyes Fanny pissing. Golden liquid between golden legs. Hoo waah!

Closet fetishists, they headed off into the jungle and were instantly in deep. Jerry pulled out a piece o' eazy skanking, and soon they were bird calling to the plush, steamy jungle, long green vines dripping with the sticky rain, trees oozed with sap. Soft squelches underneath, the quiet sound of breathing. Sharp tang of water and mud and decay and life. Jerry laid down a beat. Hard, slow, and deep. It boomed across the jungle and reverberated. A coconut fell.

Zang looked at Jerry. "What the fuck is that? You call that a beat, motherfucka? I'll show you a beat." He threw it down like this: bass down deeper than the Mariana Trench; bitch-ass MCs just keep your asses on the bench Johnny Wrench.

Fanny and Jerry burst out laughing, and a moment later, Zang was on the ground being tickled to death, and the sound of celebration rang through the jungle.

Closer in on the action, Jerry was tickling the shit out of Zang's underarms. Fanny worked his belly and sides and belly...hhaahhaaa...and her hands moved...haahahaha...like feathers...hhahaahaa...and...haaahaaha...knives tickling skittering...hahaha. And...aaaahhhh...moving lower, her right hand now rubbing and grasping and squeezing, gentle different rhythm and Zang laughing so hard and so hard, he bucked and laughed and she pumped, and oh my god, I think I have pneumothorax wowowowowowowowow! Jerry and Fanny looked at each other, smiled, and kissed, long and deep. They picked the limp Zang off the floor and continued on their way. Ah, to be alive today!

They soon found themselves back at a road and hitched a ride to Grenville. Lined up along the road, wooden and stone two-story houses and shops crowded the street. They hopped off at a corner and looked around. An arcade stood to the left, there, behind the lamppost, past the chick in the how-the-hell-did-she-get-into-that skirt. How can we get her out of it? They blinked, and she evaporated into the heat of the humid afternoon.

They entered the cave of the arcade.

Darkness utter, broken only by multicolor, flickering screens, beeping, screeching, beckoning. Shadowy figures cobraed past, hissing and whispering. "Got a quarter? Gimme a quarter?" They kept their shades on. Deeper still they plunged, a smoky hall of light and dark and pulsating shapes and throbbing sound of joysticks jerked and buttons mashed. Smoky haze of meltdown brains zapping worship, and then a door.

"I heard about this place from Johnson," Fanny whispered. Johnson, the bum with the nice shoes, the one with infinite wisdom, a hollow leg, and a palpable hatred of Rochester, New York. "This is where it happens."

Zang and Jerry didn't smile, hard motherfuckers. They knocked on the door.

"Wadded you want in deer?" Their heads whipped left. The Centipede game was talking to them. INSERT COIN flashed hypnotically at them. Jerry stepped up to the game. "Under the counter," he said, glancing skeptically at the others. They shrugged, stoned. "Can't you read da screen, mon? *Insert coin*, then."

Jerry popped two quarters into the slot and hit start. Bulbous multi-legged creatures slithered through mush-room patch toward his jism-shooting dickship as the black widow bounced around and pounced. He slid his palm over the smooth, round trackball, sliding, rolling.

"YOU A FOOL," the voice boomed. A very large man suddenly leaped out from behind the machine and grabbed them all and dragged them struggling and kicking through the door, not bothering to open it before them.

They blinked. They were standing in front of the Centipede machine, glowing INSERT COIN, and the door before them unscarred, now slightly ajar. "Fucking trip!" breathed Zang. They nodded in agreement and went in.

They found themselves on the beach, at sunset, with the golden rays of the setting sun playing across the dark, gleaming black sand. Unsurprised, they laid out a couple of towels and settled down. They each lit a fat J. The sun grew warmer, and Jerry and Zang peeled off their shirts, lying back in the sand. They each lay on either side of Fanny, who sat between them, puffing thoughtfully on her fatty. After seeing the guys pull off their shirts, Fanny thought that an excellent idea. She handed her J to Jerry and slowly lifted her T-shirt over her shoulders. Jerry and Zang watched her, as if in slow motion, as her lean, firm, rippling belly came into view, then slowly the under curve of her chest, her pert breasts covered by a spandex jog bra. As she lifted her arms over her head, the shirt covering her face, she leaned back to the ground, arching her back, thrusting her breasts up to the sky. Finally, the shirt was off, and they all let out a sigh together.

But Fanny wasn't done. Eyes still closed, she slid her hands down the sides of her body until they came to the top of her denim cutoffs. She slipped her thumbs underneath and slid them around to the snap. She slowly undid the button and, with excruciating slowness, unzipped the fly. She lifted her ass from the sand and slid the shorts over her thighs, then lifted her legs and, with them pointing straight up, kicked off her shorts. They landed crotch first on Zang's face. Fanny did the splits, running her hands down the insides of her legs until they came to the borders of her lacy boy-cut panties. Turning to Jerry, she took back her J and smiled.

Jerry leaned over to Fanny and gently kissed her. She returned the kiss, tongue swirling into his mouth. They tossed their J's aside, and Fanny pushed Jerry back down, rolling on top of him and straddling him in one quick move. Pinning his arms back behind his head, she kissed him hard, sucking and probing his mouth as she pressed her breasts into him. She rubbed her crotch against his, and as she felt his growing hard-on pressing against her, she moaned softly.

Zang watched Fanny straddling Jerry. Her ass moved hypnotically. He turned on his side, facing the passionate couple, puffing gently on his J. He watched as Jerry's hands wandered up and down Fanny's back, caressing her, then cupping and finally squeezing her ass as she rotated and thrusted it.

Fanny kissed Jerry's neck, nibbling and biting it, sliding her body slowly down him. As she moved lower, kissing and sucking his chest, he moved his hands up her side, grasping the underside of the tight spandex bra and pulling it up and off. Fanny lifted her arms to let Jerry pull off the bra. Her hard nipples and small, firm breasts pressed into Jerry's sweaty, slick, muscular belly. Fanny continued to move down Jerry's body, kissing his belly, moving her own legs up until, finally, she hovered over his shorts on all fours, her ass thrust out skyward, with the lacy panties now a thong on her taut buns. Jerry's fingers wrapped around Fanny's hair as she caressed the bulge of his hard cock with her hands. She looked up then, over at Zang, and smiled wickedly, eyes flicking down to Zang's own crotch, where the bulge of his growing cock grew more visible.

Still looking Zang in the eye, Fanny reached up and pulled down Jerry's shorts, exposing the dark-brown meat of his rigid rod, its purple head shining, curved to the left. Never taking her eyes off Zang, Fanny grasped the smooth rod and caressed it. She slowly licked it up and down, like a lollipop. Finally, she opened her lips and slowly wrapped their red fullness over the head of Jerry's throbbing cock and engulfed it.

Zang could no longer restrain himself and reached down, caressing the bulge of his own cock. Fanny smiled around Jerry's cock and started to suck and lick harder. As she watched Zang slip his hands into his shorts and saw the outline of his hand fondling and stroking the bulge of his cock, she reached down with her right hand and thrust it into her panties, caressing her moist, slick pussy. She moaned, closed her eyes, and took the full length of Jerry's cock in her mouth.

Jerry opened his eyes at the sound of Fanny's moan; he looked down to see her blonde hair splayed around his legs, her head bobbing on his cock, her hand madly working at her pussy. He glanced over at Zang, who still had a J in one hand and the other on his cock. The tip of Zang's cock just peeked out from his shorts as he caressed it. Jerry smiled.

He reached down to Fanny and started to pull her; she looked up at him. He indicated 69. She nodded and started to scoot her ass around as she sucked him, never taking her hand out of her panties. She swung her ass slowly around, giving Zang a good view all the way. As Zang watched Fanny's ass swing by, he saw her hand working madly at her pussy lips, panty crotch pushed aside. Her pussy gleamed in the sunlight. Fanny's legs slid over Zang, brushing against his crotch and chest, and he could not help but caress and squeeze her calves and thighs.

Finally, Fanny wrapped her thighs around Jerry's face. Jerry watched for a while as Fanny's fingers fondled her pussy, sliding over her clit, spreading and caressing her lips. He reached up and spread her lips, giving her hand better access to the slick, wet pussy. He finally reached out with his tongue and gently slid it across her wet, salty-sweet pussy.

She sighed and quivered. Her hand spread and pulled her lips taut, exposing the pearl of her clit. Jerry obliged and flicked it with his tongue, and she gasped, then moaned and panted as he continued to flick her clit, thus beginning a full oral assault on her pussy. Fanny threw her head back and ground her pussy into Jerry's face, thrusting and arching, jacking Jerry's shiny wet cock as she moaned. She looked over at Zang, who had tossed his J aside and now had two hands inside his shorts, jacking and stroking as he watched them. She smiled at him. Then she arched back and tapped Jerry on the head. Jerry pulled his tongue out of her pussy and looked up, lips and face shiny and wet. She nodded her head at Zang and said, "Let's get crazy!" He turned his face back into Fanny's pussy.

Zang started at the sound of Jerry's voice, hands temporarily frozen on his cock. He turned and watched as Jerry licked and sucked Fanny's pussy, watched her ass thrusting and rotating around him. He looked down to see Fanny watching him, head resting on Jerry's leg, Jerry's cock thrusting straight up in front of her. She licked Jerry's cock slowly up and down, then beckoned Zang over. Zang got up on his knees and scooted over to Fanny. His cock bulged under his shorts, just in front of her face. He looked down at her, marveling at the smooth, muscled back, watching Jerry's hands squeezing and fondling her ass as he sucked her pussy. *What a view*, thought Zang.

Fanny reached up with her hand and cupped the outline of Zang's cock through his shorts. Her excitement started to mount. She reached up and pulled the shorts down over the head of his cock. Zang slid them all the way down as his cock sprang free. Fanny looked wondrously at Zang's cock as her hand wrapped around its base. It thrust out straight, widening to a broad shoulder just below its circumcised head before narrowing slightly to its pink tip, wet with pre-cum. She had always fantasized about this, and now as she held Zang's cock in her right hand, she looked back down at Jerry's cock in her left hand, its curved length widening to a fat, purple, circumcised head. She pulled Zang closer by his cock and then slowly jacked it, kissing its shaft up and down, not using her tongue. She then slid her tongue slowly over it, marveling at how similar and different it felt from Jerry's cock, which she was stroking with her left hand. She finally wrapped her lips around Zang's throbbing hard-on and sucked it into her mouth. She felt his hands come around her head, pulling on her hair. She felt Jerry's hands tight on her ass and his tongue stabbing her as she felt more pre-cum oozing from Jerry's cock. She closed her eyes and came, moaning and sucking and grinding.

Jerry watched Fanny suck on Zang's cock and gasped. He had never seen something like this up close and live before, and the sight of Fanny's red lips and tongue swirling over his friend's cock made him hotter than he'd thought possible. No way a simple porn flick could top this. He moaned as Fanny's hand continued its slick journey up and down his own throbbing meat. Redoubling his efforts, he pulled Fanny's ass and pussy lips apart and thrust his tongue into her, fucking her with it as if it were another cock.

Zang was lost in pleasure as Fanny worked her magic on him. He ran his fingers through her golden hair, stroked her back and neck. He reached down and wrapped his fingers around one of her tits, cupping it, squeezing the hard nipple.

He almost cried out in surprise when he felt another hand on his—then he realized it was Jerry's. "Hey!" they both exclaimed.

Fanny pulled Zang's cock out of her mouth and looked back at them. "There's plenty of me to go around; you can share." They laughed.

"You like having four hands touching you?" Jerry asked.

"Yeah," breathed Fanny. "Now, get your cock back there and fuck me!"

To be continued...

Jerry Curls
January 2005

THE LAST SUPPER (IN GRENADA)
||||||||||||||||||||||||||||||||||||||||||||||||||

One day, I was walking with my friend Bob on campus when we came upon this stick. It wasn't much of a stick, really. It was just a stick lying in the grass. Being of an inquisitive nature, I picked up the stick. Normally, the act of picking up a stick would not mean anything to me. I mean, everyone picks up sticks once in a while. It's really no big deal. It's not like anyone ever talks about picking up sticks or writes about picking up sticks. Well, of course, except for right now. Why am I writing about picking up sticks, you ask? You may perhaps be thinking that this is not the most interesting subject for a short story. Ah, but make no mistake, gentle readers, for this is only the beginning of a spine-tingling tale of adventure and woe.

You see, when I actually picked up the stick, something magical happened. I'm not talking about something "magical" like in those cheesy Disney movies where the little boy turns into a prince or some crap like that. Well, actually, I am. This might sound stupid, but when I picked up that stick, I became the Wizard. I'm not talking about some wizard with a robe and a big hat who can cast spells and has magical powers. Nothing physically changed. I don't even think anything mentally changed. All I can say is that, at that moment, I knew I would be called the Wizard. My stick would become the Staff, and my friend Bob would become Bobalonius.

During this transformation, I explained it all to Bob—I mean, Bobalonius—and he understood completely. Thus, the Wizard and Bobalonius boarded the cattle truck school bus at exactly 7:00 p.m., left campus, and that's where the adventure begins.

We arrived at the home of a young Indian vixen named Sunita.

"Greetings, Sunita. How are you on this fine evening?"

"Hey, Jamz, what's up? Hey, Bob."

"Before we continue this lively conversation, Sunita, I must explain something to you. Tonight, I am known as the Wizard, and this is Bobalonius."

"Why are you a wizard?"

"I am not *a* wizard; I am *the* Wizard. I am the Wizard because I have the Staff."

"You mean that stick."

"This is not a stick. This is the Staff."

"Jams—I mean, the Wizard—can I play with your Staff?"

"Of course not. No one may lay hold of the Staff but the Wizard."

"Aw, come on, Wizard. I promise not to break it."

"Well, OK. But only if you promise not to abuse its power."

"I promise not to fondle it incorrectly. Thanks."

So I let her hold the Staff. She played with it for a little while and then proceeded to hit me on the leg with it.

"Hey, how dare you attack the Wizard with the Staff? That's my third leg. Give it back."

"No."

So we wrestled around for the Staff. She eventually cornered me and was about to maliciously and unnaturally use the powers of the Staff against me when Bobalonius gave her a traditional Middle Eastern backhand across the face and retrieved the Staff.

"Thank you, Bobalonius. And as for you, young lady, because of your wicked ways, you shall now be known as the Evil Mistry."

And so the three of us sat in the home of the Evil Mistry for a while and small talked until Clint the Cowboy showed up. Clint was from Texas and lived in the same house as Sunita. Yes, in 1995, cowboys and Indians did sometimes live together.

Being the last night in Grenada, the Evil Mistry, formerly known as Sunita, had planned a little dinner gathering at Le Bistro, the premiere French dining spot on the island. Transportation was provided by Natasha, another Indian woman. Natasha arrived in a fluorescent-pink Jeep, which was slightly louder in color than in sound.

Note: At this point in the evening, the record of events is unclear. Bobalonius and I had consumed a large amount of homemade moonshine earlier, which led to this moment of blurriness. It seemed as though Natasha would not accept a name from the Wizard. So, for the purposes of this story, her name shall reflect her taste in automobiles. She shall be known as Pinky.

And Bam! There you have it, gentle readers. Bobalonius, the Wizard, the Evil Mistry, and Pinky were on their way to Le Bistro.

Dinnertime. At this point in the evening, the record of events cannot possibly be remembered. So, so unclear. This is most probably because Bobalonius smuggled the moonshine into the restaurant and proceeded to spike the Wizard's orange juice. Besides the four characters mentioned so far, the dining table also consisted of Zarine (another Indian woman), Stephanie (a witch), and Perez the Astute.

Zarine had lost her wallet on the ride over and was fretting over it.

"Have you guys seen my wallet?"

All the alcohol had finally gotten to me, and I felt like I was about to wet myself. I rose to my feet and realized how intoxicated I really was. I grabbed the Staff for support and bumbled my way to the washroom.

And so I urinated. And what a glorious piss it was. A bright-yellow arch shooting out like a rainbow into the ceramic pond. This experience moved me. That's when I noticed a full shower stall just to the right of the urinal. What a restaurant! A shower, just in case someone shit his pants! As I reflected on this, the door to the washroom opened, and a lady half entered. But upon seeing the one-eyed snake in midstream urination, she gasped and quickly exited. I don't know who she was, but I do know that she was yet another Indian woman.

Back at the table again, I concentrated on eating some burned snails when Koorosh, the Prince of the West, showed up at our table.

"I wanted to take my lady out for a quiet dinner, but all you motherfuckers are here," he said with a grin.

"There's plenty of"—*hic*—"room for us all," I replied in a stupor.

"Man, you're wasted!"

"And you are the Prince of the West."

"Prince of the West, I like that. I feel like I should give a speech or something."

"Here, here." I banged a knife against a half glass of water to silence the crowd. "The Wizard"—*hic*—"hereby grants the Prince of the"—*hic*—"West the floor."

"All I have to say is...It was nice hangin' out with you motherfuckers, but I'm getting the fuck out of this country tomorrow. And you guys should stop the booze, weed, drugs, or whatever the fuck you're on," he said, looking at Bobalonius and me. "Catch you dogs later."

"Wise words," I answered. "A truly pious individual."

Meanwhile, Zarine still had not found her wallet and was nervously searching under the table for it.

"Have you guys seen my wallet?"

In the midst of searching for it, I broke the Staff.

"Hey, Wizard! Your Staff's gone limp. Ha-ha," laughed the Evil Mistry.

I can recall nothing else. Last brain cell is going...

Pop.

Done. Gone.

The last supper in Grenada. It was damn good.

For once.

(This story was written in its entirety aboard American Airlines, from Puerto Rico to Miami.)

December 13, 1995

LOVE?

NEW YORK CITY ROMANCE
||||||||||||||||||||||||||||||||||

Blasting off from this rock like a rocket,
Smashing anything and everything that dares sink a hope
and a dream
These thoughts propel yet backward, and most definitely
forward
To an ancient and futuristic place.
A "Lugar," stripped of cynicism, devoid of pessimism,
Shedding the shackling shell of this emotional poverty
surrounding me.

To a place where she is pure in her beauty
And I am noble in my intentions.
To a place where a man can love a woman,
Without the pestering of the he-said, she-said, should've,
could've,
Would've people.

Follow me now down a moonlit path
Through and through the darkness and the depth
Of the tall pine trees.
Away from the campfire, the music, and the smell of marsh-
mallows.

And finally here and finally now,
I am real and you are true.
And you are radiant in your smile
And sensuous in your gaze,
As you pull me down onto the forest floor.

As we slip and slide in and out of reality, in and out of fantasy,
My lifetime of loneliness groans as it hits the high road.
        I tell you, "I love you."
And you say, "Excuse me, sir, are you ready to order yet?"

May 23, 1999

THE SECOND SUNDAY OF MAY
||||||||||||||||||||||||||||||||||||||

I'm writing this letter to say, "Happy Mother's Day!"
With a poem that's supposed to rhyme,
But keep in mind, it's the first time
I'm saying "Happy Mother's Day" in a different kind of way.

As for me, med school goes on forever
And I think internal medicine
Is where I'll put my investment in.
But will I reach California? Probably never!

How's life in Orange County?
Where there's an Irani behind every tree
And everywhere the smell of ghormeh sabzi
In that land that's kind of smoggy, hot and sunny.

"Happy Mother's Day" in a poem that should be hated,
Until I reach LA and get fed,
Like Tupac said,
"Dear Mama, you are appreciated."

May 11, 1997

*B*ACHELORHOOD
||||||||||||||||||||||

Settle down? Settle down?
You should settle down.
Different girls every night,
Sometimes two or three at the same time.
Fast car, fast money, fast times,
Fast friends, a fast high
And a sloooww fuck.

Beach house
Material wealth
Tip your goblet glass of champagne
And toast to *my* health.

A white picket fence,
A dog, a cat
Blah, blah, blah
This is *your* mediocrity.

A white sack of crack,
A pad, a pen
Blazin' again and again.
This is *my* spirituality.

"Do you want to grow old alone?"
No.
But do *you* want to grow old without a soul?
Fa-mily val-ues, diamond ring
Ha-ppily ever after
Do you take her?
Yes, I do.

For rich or poor
Sure, sure.
Blah, blah...Hmphhh, hmphhh.

Breathe.

Staaaart over
Cleanse your soul.
Nothing is written
Neeeeeever mind
What you've been told.

Stop.

Christmas 2004

THE SEXY SAXOPHONE SONG
||||||||||||||||||||||||||||||||||||||||||||

I'm dancing in your womb—
I mean, your room
It's the place to be
Oh, can't you see?
My shenanigan eyes like to tickle thee
I'm thrice the size, but well inclined
And if I had a room
I could bop, bop, bop, bop

And when I want you
Under the covers
I know you want me, too.
And though we're moving
Oh, so slowly
I know you want me true.
At last, feeling flesh on my flesh
I'm fresh
To be refreshed.

So when you feel like leaving your planet,
Call me
And I *will* do the rest

November 1997

FIRST LOVE
||||||||||||||

Little fish in a big pond.
Swim, swim for your life.
The other fish ignore you,
And the fishermen don't want you.

Lonely fishy,
Where are you going?
The others swim upstream and spawn,
While you yawn your life away.

There is another world,
Or so I am told.
Let us go there, little fishy,
To be lonely together.

    Oh, fishy!
    What have you done?
    I can never forgive you.
    Good-bye.

August 19, 1993

More Than a Prozac Moment
||||||||||||||||||||||||||||||||||||||||||||||||||

No one loves me
And no one ever has
It's not that I'm ugly
I'm just horribly lonely
And you can sense that
But tonight my love
...My love...
Let my lizard unleash a lifetime of loneliness

It's not morbid and sad
Just two people having a "good time"
Bowl me over with kisses
I'll disembowel you with tongue lashes

Speak the words of romance
"Oh, baby. Oh, baby, baby, baby."
Love...? Love...?
Mmmm...I'm gonna eat you!
But still, no one loves me
And no one ever has
No one ever has

...and no one ever will.

Earth Day 1998

To Encieh
||||||||||||

Magical and I'm all about it.
Entranced in this mystical place,
1740 Winona Ryder.
Not quite a witch,
Not quite a fairy.
My four-chambered, pumping,
Sometimes-quivering heart
Has been touched.
No. Licked!
The tongue of a goddess.
Suicide?
It's not OK.
Cure the Air Thom...
Cure the Air Thom...
E, En, Enci...Miss A.
Radio in my head.
Fantasy figurine.
Paint my life on a white canvas.
Black.
I'm all about that it's not OK.

Friday the 13th, November 2004

Sleeping
||||||||||||

As I lie here on your bed
Watching you breathe,
I become intoxicated by your face
And I am unable to sleep.
Suddenly your smell has made me hungry...
And I lie here watching
And wait for you to feed me...
I am starving to taste that soft, red mouth,
And to crawl inside your sweet tongue sweet...
I crave to melt my deep, pink throat.
I wanna eat your kisses
And hold you closer...
I want to eat your warmth.
So I beckon you
And beckon you
And beg you to
Come forth.
But the silencing sounds of your deep sleep snores
Deafens my ears
And keeps telling me
Only one thing...
No,
Happy New Year.

Encieh
2005

DITCH THE VALET
|||||||||||||||||||||||

The girls ditched us for the valet
Boys, oh my God, I'm like in high
School, and this is so, so low
Class, more emotional 'cause we're coked
Up, but the direction is definitely
Down, no energy for this
Shit

"I have lost my faith in womanhood."

A long time ago.

If you're reading this, it's a mistake,
Because I don't write poems for you.

I write them for me.

October 15, 2004

SCHOOLGIRL
||||||||||||||

Wham, bam, thank you, ma'am.
Oh my God, not again
My old friend's back
Hello, Mr. Sorrow
Nice to see ya
This time the girl is Nina.

First off, girl, you're not very physical.
I won't get touched
Unless I lay naked in a bathtub
Of buffalo wings, and that sucks.

Second off, the next guy you go out—
I mean, hang out—with,
Make sure he scores high on the checklist
Just a reminder:

#1:   Is he good-looking?
#2:   Does he have a good body?
#3:   Does he make you laugh?
#4:   Is he smart?
#5:   Does he have a successful career?
#6:   Is he fun?
And of course...
#7:   Does he have a never-ending cash flow?

All of my poems are one-pagers.
"I've been hustling a long time
But I ain't got nothing."
Am I just a wanksta?

As the radio plays in the background,
"Running, running as fast as we can
I really hope we make it
We're running, keep holding my hand
So we don't get separated."

Now bring back the beat.
Nina, sometimes you can be so sweet.
Nina, sometimes you can be so mean.
And I mean I need you to believe
That we can be what you dream of in your sleep.

Palm Springs is history.
And now, with your legs up,
You can make my misery history.
Don't mean to sound scandalous,
But don't you know I planned this?

And in the end, my friend,
We can be exclusive fuck buddies.
But fuck being fuck buddies.
In the end, my friend,
I could be your boyfriend.

April Fool's Day 2003

ADAM'S EVE
||||||||||||||||

Do you remember
Those wild Friday nights
When Adam was away?

I would arrive
Just in time
With a bottle of plum wine.

We would FUCK like rabbits,
Tasting each other's juices
Well through the night.

We'd stop for a second,
Still joined at the waist,
And listen to the grind of the slippery slide.

And I'd say,   "Your husband is blind."
                  "Your husband is BLIND."

On your hands and knees, you'd squeal, "Sergio,
I am woman; hear me ROAR!"
Seven times short,
Then one thrust deep
Like wild dogs in heat.
Once, I brought a friend.
Eve, this is Jane,
And Jane, this is Eve.

I became the audience
Of the saliva-secreting
Inverted dance of the pussycats.

And she said,   "Your husband is blind."
                  "Your husband is BLIND."

Bach filled the room
As we formed a circle
And munched, munched, and munched.

Wine flowed freely
In our mouths and on the bed,
In our hair and on our FLESH.
Tongues cleaned the wine
From faces and holes,
And from bellies and poles.

Old Faithful was I
As Adam barged into the place,
And my liquid shot into his face.

And he said,   "Your husband is blind."
                 "Your husband is BLIND!"

February 1995

ETHICS, PART I

||||||||||||||||||||||

Of all the kisses
I've played make-believe before
She was the tortured, ravenous,
Starving red rose.
Sterling indefinite
Unrequited breathless
Panting like breathing
Breath and alone
One tiny flower in time
Caught in our trenches
Caught in our darkness
Caught in a bed, crying...
Blissful and torn...

Encieh
November 28, 2006

Nights like That (after our first kiss)
||||||||||||||||||||||||||||||||||||||||||||||||||||

I wore that underwear for days
Because it still smelled like that night,
And I would smile
As I smelled it.
The ocean and your voice,
Drunken with poetry,
DRUNKEN RED POETRY.
And I didn't want to wash you
Out of my hair.
And I could actually allow this smell to stay,
But I washed it off anyway,
Because nights like that must always end.
Because nights like that could never stay.

Encieh
September 2004

CANDLELIGHT
||||||||||||||||||

Can you sleep tonight?
Without my hand cupping your breast
And my chest for your head to rest.
Breakfast in bed?
No. Order Chinese food to go instead
These words flow freely now
Finally free from your foolishness
Less than a pleasure it has been
Now, you can't kick me in the back
Steal the blankets or push me off the bed again
True, this voyage was forced, of course.
Clinging to a dream
Like building a house on a foundation of marshmallows.
Flickering shadows
Like a candle in a tornado
Show me the way now.
Will I explode?
My smooth, soothing voice
Replaced by the sound of a Smith & Wesson
That's easy to load.
This bird has flown.
As I sit alone
Writing this poem in the candlelight,
I ask you yet again
Can you sleep tonight?

October 1999

ONLY I KNOW
|||||||||||||||||

The man stood anxiously waiting while the woman fumbled with the strings around the box. This moment had been long overdue, and finally, with one last snip of string, the box was open. Upon seeing the contents of the box, the woman licked her lips, leaving them glistening and wet, ready to devour.

FANTASY #20
||||||||||||||||||||

She leans back on the dining table. All the food starts to burn. He moves to her and mounts her in missionary position on the dining table. He puts her legs up and calls her "Angelica." She tickles his butt and calls him "Benny the Frog."

They grind and grind on the marble dining table, while the pineapple upside-down cake and pot roast burn. This was their first time—well, at least together.

She wants to stop drinking. She thinks she's an alcoholic. Little Angelica, an alcoholic. But tonight she's going on the wagon. Sex is the answer. She's gonna trade alcohol for sex. Every time we do it, it's like a drink.

Come on, have a drink of this.

September 14, 2004

THE METROSEXUAL
||||||||||||||||||||||||

I don't write poems anymore.
It's not that I don't want to...
It's just that no one cares to read them.

Poor baby me.
But once in a while,
My soul goes into labor.
And somehow, words are delivered.

Like tonight.
It's raining.
Darkness, but the candle is flickering.
Moaning—no, not me...
The neighbors are fucking.

I am the metro-hetero-sexual antisocial.
"If you don't know, now you know."

Put me in a robe
And send me for a facial.
This is the VIP-attending lifestyle.
Drop the baggage
And step into the game.

Ding, ding. Round one.
It's little miss overworked and underpaid
Versus the metrosexual.

Midnight, February 26, 2004

THE GYPSY CAFÉ
||||||||||||||||||||||

One word: cozy.
Snuggled deep within the mirth,
  The laughter, the camaraderie,
  The tables and chairs, the coffee,
  The croissants, the paintings, the music,
  The noise of the cappuccino maker,
  The textbooks and the highlighters;
    I studied the human body
    And all of its intricacies.

The warmth of humans,
Packed into a small room.
Outside, a cold old man,
  With guitar in one hand and
  Sleeping bag in the other
    Talks with snacking sidewalk patrons.

Flirting eyes gaze, penetrate the thick, musky air
  And entwine two bodies like vines.
A man with a professor's beard and glasses
  Buys an espresso for a woman,
  Who resembles a paper goddess
    From the pages of *Cosmopolitan*.

Histology,
"Is that the study of history?" she asks.
"Is that the study of her-story?" I reply
  As I read of menstruation and ovulatory cycles,
  Endometriosis and estrogen, fertilization and embryos.

Finally, after hours of brain and social expansion,
      The last song ends, and the last chair is flipped.

Outside, the icy winter air is so very cold...

February 1994

VAN GOGH'S EAR
||||||||||||||||||||||||

Whisked away once again
By the icy-cold fingers of night.
Estranged and entranced
Into the oLD lADY's shoe.

A two-story shack.
Mirth, camaraderie, and the love of food.
Van Gogh lost his ear.
Westwood lost its heart.

To Jane

April 1994

THE CHAIRLIFT
||||||||||||||||

Now I'm alone on the chairlift.
Finally, the people have gone.
Three inches of snow on my thighs.
My ski poles married to my gloves.

One hundred feet above the ground,
My skis cut through the black liquid of night.
My lungs, all frosty with ice,
My nose does the drip-and-drip.

Ten ice cubes pass for fingers.
There's no one on this chairlift.
Tonight, it's just me and the mountain.
The blizzard rapes my face.

Heed my little warning.
I'd rather be on this chairlift,
Where the night is cold and real,
Than to be in your loving tentacles.

You see, your love, it stings like a scorpion.
When I'm with you, I feel like I'm poisoned, dying.
Out here, I am so alive.
Out here, I'll live forever.

Otherwise, I'm already dead.
Can you touch my frozen ears?
You should, because you put them there.
Good-bye, fucked-up planet.

June 4, 1992

A Night in Heaven
||||||||||||||||||||||||||||

So many years
Finally, I am free.
Not forever,
But at least for tonight.

The fools, the witches,
You'll miss me tonight.
I am free from your cruelty.
Happy.

I am silly, naive, softhearted.
Only tonight.
My heart and mind are open (ready to be stepped on)
Only tonight.

Even now, my words wish to slip away from the page.
I write like a love-stricken little girl.
Ah, the innocence, the beauty.
Happy.

This night and others like it.
This is what keeps my sanity.
And when this night is gone,
My sanity, likewise, will follow.

I know a certain someone saved my life tonight.
Happy.
I know a certain someone will eventually cause my death.
History repeats itself.

June 25, 1992

MORE THAN A FRIEND
||||||||||||||||||||||||||||

Sunset.
The night shrouds us, crowds us
And so begin the music
Entertain us.

One bloody mary.
For me, some drink with a cherry
Luxurious lounge lays out time
Languidly.

On the street
Hold my hand
And jump in the yellow limousine
On our way
Apartment 14.

House of Lunacy
Cozy, snuggled up like babies
Time for the real fun
But first, Channel 81.

Love or lust?
God's sweat, thrusting with no end.
Sunrise.
I'm more than a friend.

October 1999

196

THE REFUNDED TICKET
||||||||||||||||||||||||||||||||

Hey, hey, hey,
What can I say?
Just wanted to talk to my girl from around the way,
The one who used to give me play.

But to my dismay,
Two days from today,
I should have been out there by the Bay
For Thanksgiving, but what can I say?

November 19, 1997

ONE-NIGHT STANDOFF

|||||||||||||||||||||||||||||

Time is not on our side.
As we sit side by side,
Let the night slip idly by.
And we shake hands good-bye.

Sleep tonight,
But leave on the light.
All will be just right.
I can't put up a fight.

Tick-tock, tick-tock
Stubborn, pushy little clock
  Bend me but don't break me.
  Grasping, grasping, but still alive.
  Do you know me? Do you know me?

  My soul has been ripped out of my young body and
  thrown into a subway train.

Time is not on our side.
Today will last forever,
Or until you say good-bye.

December 6, 1997

*U*NTITLED (*WHEN OUT...BY SANAZ*)

||||||||||||||||||||||||||||||||||||||||||||||||

When out, others
Scream at my deaf
Soul to dance
They do not know that without
You I cannot, that any movement
Would betray the rhythm our souls composed.

-Sanaz
September 2004

A DEMON NAMED CUPID
IIIIIIIIIIIIIIIIIIIIIIIIIIIIIIII

I'm down; can you feel the sweat on my brow?
I'm touched; they say love is such a rush.
At last, I've found a way to forget my past.
Crazy girl, take a trip through and into my world.

Hail to you, the queen of spite and gloom.
Spellbound, with a forked tongue you wear your crown.
Give and take, feigned kindness in the laugh you fake.
Blushed red, and forever, that's what you said.

A life cut short with the deadly knife.
Brain dead, the chills flow from toe to head.
Foolish, how I loved, oh, such a bitch.
Good-bye, my blood tears are long since dry.

Every day and in every way, my stroked-out brain.
My emotion potion in your ocean, not today.
I gave my blood and opened up, you spat in my face.
I've lost all pride and will to live; it's just like rape.

A demon
A demon named Cupid
Just for two
But not for me

A demon
A demon named Cupid
I died for you
And then you shat on me.

1990

CALGON, TAKE ME AWAY
||||||||||||||||||||||||||||||||||

Sweet, sweet, SWEET sweat on my brow
Cook me NOW hot sun
Simmer ME down
'Cause I ain't the one

Wet, luscious leaves of grass
Whisk me away to the land of ebony
Let her be, let her be
My casualties on display like tapestries

Hear me, smell me, touch me, see me
BELIEVE me
In my big brown eyes
Ah, this shit's killin' me

Surf and sand, faraway land
With the top down
Sippin', dippin', just straight rollin'
I'm a baller in a world of imposters

Home, sweet home, and I've said it
Red eyes, an empty bed
My friends are dead
And Benny boy's had it.

December 6, 1997

37 REASONS WHY
||||||||||||||||||||||||||||

Talk is cheap.
Shut up and kiss me.

December 6, 1997

I WILL NEVER FORGET THE SORROW

I will never forget the sorrow,
As I lie wide-eyed and terrified
In the darkest hours of the night
With no one to comfort or hold tight.

I will never forget the sorrow
Of so many years, beyond child's tears
A screaming animal of sadness
Dancing with the fringes of madness.

I will never forget the sorrow.
The ugly and fat, with them I sat.
In pure torment every day of life.
To be each other's sad groom and wife.

I will never forget the sorrow.
To look in her eyes, eyes full of lies
Lost once again in a cold embrace
 Till another time, another place

I will never forget the sorrow.
Just to be held, and to feel life, and
To be in bliss for one moment, and
To bask on the warm beach, hand in hand.

I will never forget the sorrow.
Always filled with hate, this is my fate.
I am love repellant, so she says
I believe she's right, I must confess.

I will never forget the sorrow.
The moans from next door, she screams for more.
Trapped in my body coffin, I lay.
Choking in my own pity, I pray.

I will never forget the sorrow.
Just a glimpse of hope, or use the rope.
I must believe I'll get to that beach,
Rope and the sand, both still in my reach.

I will never forget.

June 5, 1992

INSPIRATION
||||||||||||||||||||||||||||||

QUOTABLES
||||||||||||||

"Life was fun while it lasted."
    —Eric "Eazy-E" Wright

"Loneliness is not a phase."
    —Alice in Chains

"In the abundance of water, the fool is thirsty."
    —Bob Marley

"Never tell me the odds."
    —Han Solo

"Every brother ain't a brother, 'cause a black hand squeezed the life out of Malcolm X, man."
    —Public Enemy

"A fear of weapons is a sign of retarded sexual and emotional maturity."
    —Sigmund Freud

"Strangest feelin' I'm feelin'
But Jah love we will always believe in
Though you may think my faith is in vain
Till Shiloah reach I, rastafari's name."
    —Buju Banton

"I see Death around the corner."
    —Tupac Shakur

"When the dust begins to settle from the windstorm of my day, I like to chill out with a smooth cool glass of Chardonnay."
    —Ben Zandpour, MD

"I got so much game, I need a referee."
    —Ice Cube

"I wasn't born with enough middle fingers."
    —Marilyn Manson

"Most people keep their brains between their legs."
    —Steven Patrick Morrissey

"There is no body cavity that cannot be reached with a #14 needle and a good, strong arm."
    —Samuel Shem, MD

"The capital of the United States is not Washington. It's Tel Aviv."
    —Mohammad Khatami, President of Iran

"Bitch, you know the side. World muthafuckin' wide."
    —Westside Connection

"I wish they all could be California girls."
    —The Beach Boys

"Machiavelli's chief contribution to political thought lies in his freeing political action from moral considerations...he was not a scholar and he did not have the temperament of one who finds knowledge an end in itself. Knowledge for him was a springboard for the deed."
    —Daniel Donno

Quotes from The Smiths

IIIIIIIIIIIIIIIIIIIIIIIIIIIIIIIIIIIII

"I need advice, I need advice
Because nobody ever looks at me twice."

"Pretty girls make graves."

"Sorrow's native son,
He will not rise for anyone."

"I lost my faith in Womanhood."

"There are brighter sides to life
And I should know because I've seen them
But not very often..."

"Am I still ill?"

LIFE GOES ON
||||||||||||||||||

How many brothers fell victim to the streets
Rest in peace young nigga, there's a heaven for a G
Be a lie, if I told ya that I never thought of death
My nigga, we the last ones left
But life goes on

How many brothers fell victim to the streets
Rest in peace young nigga, there's a heaven for a G
Be a lie, if I told ya that I never thought of death
My nigga, we the last ones left
Life goes on

[Verse One]

As I bail through the empty halls
Breath stinkin' in my jaws
Ring, ring, ring, quiet y'all, incoming call
Plus this my homie from high school, he gettin' by
It's time to bury another brother, nobody cry
Life as a baller, alcohol and booty calls
We used to do them as adolescents, do you recall?
Raised as Gs, loc'ed out and blazed the weed
Get on the roof let's get smoked out and blaze with me
Two in the morning and we still high assed out
Screamin' thug till I die before I passed out
But now that you're gone, I'm in the zone
Thinkin' I don't wanna die all alone
But now ya gone
And all I got left are stinkin' memories
I love them niggas to death, I'm drinkin' Hennessy

While tryin' to make it last
I drank a fifth for that ass when you passed
'Cause life goes on

Yeah nigga I got the word as hell
Ya blew trial and the judge gave you 25 with an L
Time to prepare to do fed time won't see parole
Imagine life as a convict that's gettin' old
Plus with the drama we're lookin' out for your baby's mama
Takin' risks, while keepin' cheap tricks from gettin' on her
Life in the hood is all good for nobody
Remember gamin' on dumb hotties at chill parties
Me and you no true a two
While scheming on hits and gettin' tricks
That maybe we can slide into
But now you buried
Rest nigga 'cause I ain't worried
Eyes blurried, sayin' good-bye at the cemetery
Though memories fade
I got your name tatted on my arm
So we both ball till my dyin' days
Before I say good-bye
Kato and Mental rest in peace
Thug till I die

Bury me smilin', with Gs in my pocket
Have a party at my funeral, let every rapper rock it
Let the hoes that I used to know
From way before
Kiss me from my head to my toe
Give me a paper and pen
So I can write about my life of sin
A coupla bottles of gin in case I don't get in

Tell all my people I'm a Ridah
Nobody cries when we die
We outlaws let me ride
Until I get free
I live my life in the fast lane got police chasin' me
To my niggas from old blocks from old crews
Niggas that guided me through back in the old school
Pour out some liquor have a toast for the homies
See we both gotta die but you chose to go before me
And brothers miss you while you're gone
You left your nigga on his own, how long we moan
Life goes on

Life goes on homie
Gone on, 'cause they passed away
Niggas doin' life
Niggas doin' fifty and sixty years and shit
I feel ya nigga, trust me, I feel ya
You know what I mean
Last year
We poured out liquor for you
This year nigga, life goes on
We're gonna clock now
Get money, evade bitches, evade tricks
Give players plenty space
And basically just represent for you baby
Next time you see your niggas
You're gonna be on top nigga
They gonna be like,
Goddamn, them niggas came up
That's right baby
Life goes on
And we up out this bitch

Hey Kato, Mental
Y'all niggas make sure it's poppin' when we get up there man
Don't front

How many brothers fell victim to the streets
Rest in peace young nigga, there's a heaven for a G
Be a lie, if I told ya that I never thought of death
My nigga, we the last ones left
But life goes on

—Tupac Shakur

I JACKED VOLTAIRE
||||||||||||||||||||||||||

Men were originally fish.

You despise books, you whose whole life is devoted to the vanities of ambition and the search for pleasure, or plunged in idleness; but you should realize that the whole of the known world, with the exception of the savage races, is governed by books alone.

If you have a lawsuit, your goods, your honor, your very life depends on the interpretation of a book that you never read.

Men can only have a certain number of teeth, hair and ideas. There comes a time when he necessarily loses his teeth, his hair and his ideas.

Friendship is the marriage of souls, and this marriage is subject to divorce.

It should be noted that only men, turtle-doves, and pigeons, are acquainted with kisses.

Sheep live very placidly together, and they are considered very easy going, because we do not see the prodigious quantity of animal they devour.

There is no king comparable to a cock.

No country has a good code of laws.

Ants are considered to be excellent democrats.

We resemble the monkeys more than any other animal...

Why should we lock up a man or woman who chooses to walk stark naked in the street?

You do not know what nature is.

The world is the theater of moral Ill and physical Ill.

KILLAH HILLS 10304

||||||||||||||||||||||||||

Life of a drug dealer
Killah Hills, 10304

Restaurants on a stake-out
So order the food take out
Payoff outside a sport steakhouse
Maintain the power, I feel the deal's goin' sour
Nigga Mr. West, late a fuckin' half hour
And his man who bought land from Tony Starks
While he was contractin' bricklayin' jobs in city parks
He's a loan shark, can't just raise a gram to a finger
In a garment that's stretched, got it sewn like Singer
Is all I talk blasphemy? this kid after me
For the heist—dead relative—co-faculty
Fuck it, he turned states on my nigga
Cash flow this cold polly
Who used to drop white sacks of blow on his ve'cle
Here I'll be labeled death as I land
200 pounds south from Thailand
Right off the docks,
I got the luxurious custom made yachts
Burying plots, for my niggaz hit with baby shots
There's no need for us to spray up the scene
I use less men, more powerful shit for my team
Like my man Mohammed from Afghanistan
Grew up in IRAN
The nigga runs a neighborhood newsstand
A wild Middle Eastern, bomb specialist
Initiated at eleven to be a terrorist
He sent bombs in bottles of champagne

And when niggaz popped the cork
niggaz lost half their brains
Like this expert who tried to smuggle a half a key
in his left leg, even underwent surgery
They say his pirate limp gave him away
As the feds rushed him, comin' through US Customs
Now look who's on the witness stand singin'
a well-known soprano
A smash hit from Sammy Rivano
here's the plan—minimum for the hit—two hundred grand
Have to time everything blast the nigga out o' the stands
The sharp shooters hit the prosecutor
The judges were sent Photographs of their wives takin' baths
Along with briefcase filled with 1.5
that's the bribe
Take it or commit suicide
1st rule: anyone who sleeps on the golden cereal
I want they small intestines ripped from their interior
I got a price for those jewels, shipped from freight cargo
Don't forget to launder the green through Wells Fargo
Being struck for process and plans for the call
To Costa Rica 400 barrels of ether
200 pounds of reefer
and fifty immigrants with fake Visas

Life of a drug dealer
Killah hills, 10304
The saga continues

—Genius/Gza
(Wu-tang Clan)

I've Changed My Plea to Guilty

||||||||||||||||||||||||||||||||||||||||||||||

I'm standing in the dark
With my innocent hand on my heart.
I've changed my plea.
I've changed my plea to guilty,
Because freedom is wasted on me.
See how your rules spoil the game.

Outside there is a pain.
Emotional air raids exhausted my heart,
And it's safer to be inside.
So, I'm changing my plea.
And no one can dissuade me,
Because freedom was wasted on me.
See how your rules spoil the game.

Something I have learned,
If there is one thing in life I've observed,
It's that everybody's got somebody.
Ooh no, not me.
So I've changed my plea to guilty.
And reason and freedom are wasted...

—Morrissey

I KNOW IT'S GONNA HAPPEN SOMEDAY
||||||||||||||||||||||||||||||||||||||||||||||||||

My love,
Wherever you are,
Whatever you are,
Don't lose faith.
I know it's gonna happen someday to you.

Please wait.
Please wait.
Wait.
Don't lose faith.

You say that day
Just never arrives,
And it's never seemed so far away.
Still, I know it's gonna happen someday to you.

Please wait.
Don't lose faith.

—Morrissey

PLEASE, PLEASE, PLEASE, LET ME GET WHAT I WANT

||||||||||||||||||||||||||||||||||||

Good times for a change
See the luck I've had
Would make a good man
Turn bad
So please, please, please
Let me, let me, let me
Let me get what I want
This time

Haven't had a dream in a long time
See the life I've had
Would make a good man bad
So, for once in my life
Let me get what I want
Lord knows it would be the first time
Lord knows it would be the first time

—The Smiths

WELL I WONDER
||||||||||||||||||||||

Well I wonder
Do you hear me when you sleep?
I hoarsely cry.

Well I wonder
Do you see me when we pass?
I half die.

Please keep me in mind.
Please keep me in mind.

Gasping, but somehow still alive.
This is the final stand of all I am.

Gasping, dying, but somehow still alive
This is the final stand of all I am.

Please keep me in mind

—The Smiths

SWEET AND TENDER HOOLIGAN
||||||||||||||||||||||||||||||||||||||||||||

So, I walked into this dark and dreary Irish pub in Beverly Hills on a bright Tuesday afternoon. A few scattered souls were brewing about, some at the bar, some at booths. I sat next to this British fellow who was in his midforties—receding hairline, wearing mostly black, mumbling to himself, and swirling a drink.

The bartender's look told me I wasn't supposed to be there, but after I ordered my beer, he went about his business. I introduced myself to the Brit.

"Hello, there. My name is Ben."

The guy looked me over, as if I shouldn't have been there, but then he stuck out his hand.

"I'm Steven. Pleased to meet you."

And so I sat there for the next five minutes without saying a word, just watching the soundless TV at the bar.

All of a sudden, the Brit put down his drink and turned toward me. "So, what do *you* do, Mr. Ben?"

"I'm a doctor."

"Ahh! A doctor! And what kind of doctor are you, Mr....Dr. Ben?"

"Internal medicine."

"And what is that exactly?"

"Well, it's like an adult doctor. I don't take care of kids or deliver babies. Or do surgery."

"I see. I've been told I don't get enough vitamin B12 in my diet."

"You must be a vegetarian...?"

His expression told me I should have known.

I continued, "You see, vitamin B12 is the only vitamin exclusively found in animal products. You can get iron from beans and dark green vegetables, calcium from broccoli, et cetera, but there's no way around B12."

"Really..." Steven sat back in his chair. "How can someone so young speak words so wise?"

"Well, thank you."

One of the men sitting at a booth came over and spoke with a British accent.

"Excuse me, Moz. We have to get to that *Spin* interview."

"Right. Right," Steven replied. He turned toward me and continued, "Dr. Ben, it was a pleasure meeting you. Perhaps I can ask you for more medical advice in the future. I don't really have a doctor."

"Sure. Here's my card. Feel free to give me a ring."

"Do you give your card to everyone?" Steven asked.

"No. Only to the unlovable."

As Steven walked out with his entourage, he turned around. "Oh, by the way, Ben, I'm just curious. Do you know who I am?"

I looked at him blankly, my best poker face.

"Yes, you're Steven. A British guy with vitamin B12 deficiency."

He chuckled. Then he laughed hard, like he hadn't laughed in a long time. Then he walked out.

And that is how I became friends with Morrissey.

September 4, 2004

THE END

MACHIAVELLI QUOTABLES

|||||||||||||||||||||||||||||||||

"When there is no distinction of custom, men will live quietly."

"Anyone who conquers such territories and wishes to hold onto them must do two things: the first is to extinguish the ruling family; the second is to alter neither the laws nor the taxes."

"Being on the spot, one may observe disorders as they arise and quell them quickly; not being present, one will learn about them only when they have assumed such proportions that they cannot be quelled."

"In the beginning the disease is easy to cure but hard to diagnose; with the passage of time, having gone unrecognized and unmedicated, it becomes easy to diagnose but hard to cure."

"He who causes another to become powerful ruins himself, for he brings such a power into being either by design or by force, and both of these elements are suspect to the one whom he has made powerful."

"People are by nature changeable."

"Like all things in nature that spring up and grow quickly, states that come hastily into being cannot have proper roots and branches."

"If one has unusual ability and does not lay the foundations beforehand, he can lay them afterward, though with trouble for the architect and danger to the edifice."

"A man who strives after goodness in all his acts is sure to come to ruin."

"Love endures by a bond which men, being scoundrels, may break whenever it serves their advantage to do so; but fear is supported by the dread of pain, which is ever present."

"A prince—especially a prince who has but recently attained power—cannot observe all of those virtues for which men are reputed good, because it is often necessary to act against mercy, against faith, against humanity, against frankness, against religion in order to preserve the state."

"A conspirator cannot act alone."

"Princes are inescapably exposed to assassinations of the king which are the work of desperate men."

"Nothing is so weak and unstable as a reputation for power which is not based on one's own strength."

—Niccolo Machiavelli, Circa 1512

THE SWEETEST THING
||||||||||||||||||||||||||||

My love she throws me like a river—more
The sweetest thing.
She won't catch me or break my fall
The sweetest thing.
Baby's got blue skies up ahead, but in this I'm a rain cloud
You know she like a dry kind of love
The sweetest thing.

I'm losing you ain't love the sweetest thing?

I wanted to run but she made me crawl
The sweetest thing.
It turns to fire, she turned me to straw
The sweetest thing.
I know I got black eyes, but they burn so brightly for her
Mine is a blind kind of love
The sweetest thing.

I'm losing you, ain't love the sweetest thing?

Blue-eyed boy meets a brown-eyed girl
The sweetest thing.
You can sew it up but you still see the tip
The sweetest thing.
Baby's got blue skies up ahead, and in this I'm a rain cloud
You know we got a stormy kind of love

The sweetest thing.

—U2

227

MANNISH BOY
||||||||||||||||||

Oh yeah!
Oh yeah!

Everything gonna be alright this mornin'

Now when I was a young boy,
At the age of five
My mother said I'm a be
The greatest man alive.
But now I'm a man.
I make twenty-one.
I want you believe me honey,
we have lots of fun.
I'm a man
I spell "M"..... "A" chil'..... "N."
That represents "man."
No "B"..... "O" chil'..... "Y."
That spells mannish boy
But man,
I'm a full grown man.
I'm a man.
I'm a rollin' stone

- Muddy Waters

In My Life
||||||||||||||

There are places I'll remember all my life,
Though some have changed,
Some forever, not for better,
Some have gone and some remain.

All these places had their moments
With lovers and friends I still can recall.
Some are dead and some are living.
In my life I've loved them all.

But of all these friends and lovers,
There is no one compares with you.
And these memories lose their meaning
When I think of love as something new.

Though I know I'll never lose affection
For people and things that went before
I know I'll often stop and think about them
In my life I love you more

Though I know I'll never lose affection
For people and things that went before
I know I'll often stop and think about them
In my life I love you more
In my life I love you more

—The Beatles

WAR
||||||

Until the philosophy
Which holds one race superior
And another inferior
Is finally and permanently
Discredited and abandoned,
Everywhere is war.

Until there are no longer
First class and second class
Citizens of any nation,
Until the color of a man's skin
Is of no more significance
Than the color of his eyes,
Is War.

Until the basic human rights
Are equally granted to all
Without regard to race
It's war.

Until that day,
The dream of lasting peace,
World citizenship,
Rule of international morality
Will be but a fleeting illusion,
To be pursued but never obtained.
Everywhere is war.

Until the ignoble and unhappy regimes
that hold our brothers
In Angola, In Mozambique,
South Africa
In sub-human bondage
Have been toppled,
Totally destroyed,
Everywhere is war.

War in the east,
War in the west,
War up north,
War down south—
War rumors of a war.

And until that day,
The African continent
Will not know peace.
We Africans will fight.
We find it necessary.
And we know we shall win,
As we are confident
In the victory of good over evil

Good over evil

War.

—Bob Marley

Quickies!
||||||||||||

"I've never read anything like this. It's kind of 'counter-culture'...I suppose you can try taking it to *Playboy* or the Howard Stern show, but I can't help you."
—Seven Locks Press

"I can't believe this guy made it through medical school. I wonder what he's done with his life. What's this interview for again?"
—O. Vesal, MD

"Although this book seems silly and tongue-in-cheek, upon second reading, a handful of philosophical, social, moral, and ethical themes present themselves."
—Anonymous

"I liked it, but it's kind of weird...different. Pokingly unique."
—The author's sister

"I'm like...I mean...I liked it. It's unusual for someone in a science field to have any redeeming qualities."
—The author's sister's roommate

ABOUT THE AUTHOR

||||||||||||||||||||||||||||

DJ Ass Maggots is a pseudonym for a doctor practicing internal medicine with an emphasis on geriatric care somewhere in Southern California. He lives a lifestyle of excess that would make most of his peers jealous—that is, if they knew. When he was born, when he will die, *where* he was born, and where he grew up are really not that important, but most authors display these facts on the back cover of their books. Well, if you really want to know, he received his MD in 1998 and his Internal Medicine Board Certification in 2001. He now practices hospital medicine and is the medical director of several medical facilities.

But don't hold that against him.

www.ingramcontent.com/pod-product-compliance
Lightning Source LLC
Chambersburg PA
CBHW060137130626
46556CB00006B/2379